# TWO CHRISTMAS PICKLES

## A MULBURY MYSTERY NOVELLA

### JUNO HARVEY

First published by Mandurang Press 2023

Book cover by Melissa Williams Design

ISBN: 978 0 6452604 9 6 (ebook)

ISBN: 978 0 6456511 2 6 (paperback)

*To those who spent Christmas in the rain*

# ONE

The rumbling made Rosemary Exeter pause with her finger pressed against the tape holding the Cracker Christmas Kids Charity flyer in position on the window of her shop, The Preserved Mulbury. She waited. The noise waned and disappeared. 'Thunder, not motorbikes, Sunny,' she said to the ginger tabby sitting on the windowsill below. The cat stirred her tail but kept her gaze on the outside world. *Well, I could have told you that,* she seemed to say. *Look at that sky.*

It was eleven o'clock on Christmas Eve and yet the day was shrouded in grey. Heavy clouds hung over the little Australian tourist town of Mulbury, roiling with unfallen rain. Visitors scurried across Goldmarket Square squinting up at the sky and holding their precious purchases of jams, lavender soaps, and second-hand books to their chests. Kelly Flanagan was outside Mullings of Mulbury folding up the large umbrellas she kept over her café tables as shade, and putting them away hastily, while Rakisha at The Sweet Potato stacked the rattan chairs she had in the Square into sets of four, and then struggled to lift them.

Rosemary sighed. Although she wouldn't venture out to help Kelly unless it was an emergency, she couldn't leave Rakisha to heave a load of chairs inside her café, perhaps tripping on her flowing garments and falling. She opened her jangling door and crossed Goldmarket Road. 'Rakisha,' she said. 'Let me.'

Rakisha stopped her efforts to lift the load of chairs, and flung her long, grey ringlets over her shoulders. 'Oh, Rosemary, darling, you've come just at the right time.' She held out a bangled arm and wriggled her fingers. 'It's starting.'

Rosemary didn't have to ask what she meant. The clouds had cracked open, letting large drops of water fall heavily to the parched ground. She picked up the stack of chairs. 'You open the door of the café and I'll put them inside.'

Rakisha turned a radiant face to her friend. 'What was that, darling?'

'The door, Rakisha. Open the door.'

Rakisha shook her head as if just waking up. 'Yes, yes. Isn't it wondrous to feel nature's moisturise on your skin after all this time?'

'It would be,' said Rosemary, hoisting the chairs up a little, 'if I wasn't holding four chairs in my arms.'

Rakisha blinked at the chairs and jumped. 'Oh, sorry, darling.' She scuttled to the door of The Sweet Potato, tie-dyed layers catching at her ankles, and pulled it open. 'It's been such a hot start to summer, I was momentarily lost in the moment. Aren't you feeling a little scorched, too, darling?'

Rosemary didn't answer until all the chairs were safely out of the weather and she had shut the door. Rakisha stood in the now teeming rain while Rosemary stayed in the protection of the eave above the door. 'Scorched like an almond,' she said, although Rakisha was doing a jig on the gravel and didn't hear.

It had been a dry few months, with temperatures high even for an Australian summer. The last decent rain was a distant memory, and the residents of Mulbury were on self-imposed water restrictions. It was a common sight for people to be seen carrying buckets of shower water out to the pot plants in front of their shops and houses and tipping them ever-so-carefully in so as not to spill a drop. Rosemary looked at Rakisha dancing in the rain, thunder menacing overhead, and smiled at her elation.

The rain pulled people out of their shops one by one. Over the road, the faint croak of an electronic motion sensor frog sounded as Mrs Lionel stepped out of The Green Mulbury and went to stand near a veranda post. She waved at Rosemary and pointed to Rakisha, but Rosemary could only shrug. Jasper Lu came out of his bookshop and stood next to the older woman; his expression puzzled. By the time Gerry and Patti came out of their upcycled garment shop, Patricia's, Mrs Lionel had clearly explained Rakisha's view of rain to him because Rosemary saw Jasper's face relax as he nodded.

Rakisha kept dancing, her colourful layers flapping wetly and Rosemary left her to it. She ran back across Gold-market Road and under the veranda, where she squeezed out her silver-streaked braid.

'Quite a puddle you're making there, dear,' said Mrs Lionel, peering down at the path. 'We haven't had a down-fall like for quite some years.'

'I've never seen anything like it,' said Jasper, coming over to Rosemary and offering her a clean hanky to wipe her face. 'And I've been here for at least five years.'

'I remember that flash flood we had,' said Gerry. 'A long

time ago now, before Patricia's was up and running. You remember that, too, Patti?'

His wife nodded, bouncing a little on her toes. 'Oh, yes. We'd just bought the shop. We were only going to live in it, weren't we? Not turn it into a business.'

'Funny how it goes,' said Jasper. 'We think we're going to do one thing and then...'

A roll of thunder drowned out his next words. Rosemary tipped her head. Not thunder this time but the drone of motorcycles coming into town, the sound a deepening rumble until a fleet turned the corner from Big Town and pulled into Goldmarket Square. Patti covered her ears from the noise while Rosemary counted the machines in front of her. Six in total, two with sidecars.

'What is this?' shouted Gerry, as the rain belted down harder on the tin roof of the veranda. 'A bikie gang?'

'Not a gang.' Rosemary pointed as the last bike halted, and its rider kicked down the stand. 'See the sign?'

Drab though it was in the dark rain, a stiff banner on an angled stick poking from the rider's pannier gave the game away: Cracker Christmas Kids' Charity Run.

'Oh, I see,' said Mrs Lionel. 'They're collecting for Cracker Christmas Kids.'

'Collecting what?' said Jasper.

'Presents. They're the mobile collection riders. The public give them the presents, they wrap them up, and then they'll be the delivery riders, taking presents to a depot for distribution to children whose families can't afford to buy any.'

'A noble cause,' said Gerry. 'I hope the presents stay dry, though. I bet they weren't expecting weather like this.'

Rosemary studied the motorcycles. Most were sophisticated road bikes, their panniers large and secure. The two sidecars held enormous taupe-coloured sacks that bulged with odd shapes. As the riders dismounted, they pointed with concern at their loads.

'They don't look like your typical charity types,' said Gerry.

'Gerry, don't be boring,' said Patti, cupping her coiled apricot hair. 'What does a typical charity type look like?'

'Not sure. But I didn't expect them to have such long beards.'

He was right there. As each rider took off their helmets, their beards were exposed. Some hung down to their middles, the rain pulling each straight. A couple were sensibly braided, probably to keep them from tangling, Rosemary reasoned. As one rider turned his back to the crowd under the veranda to talk to his mates, she saw the words on his leather jacket: The Bearded Biker Brothers.

The rain eased. Rakisha, who'd continued to dance despite the influx of motorcycles, stopped mid-flutter, her arms outstretched and her head tipped back. One of the men approached her but didn't seem to know what to say. 'I'll go and see what they want,' said Rosemary. 'I'm already drenched.'

'Good idea, dear,' said Mrs Lionel. 'They might be our last visitors today. I don't think people will want to be Mulbury tourists on such a sodden day.'

Rosemary jumped the streaming gutter and made her way back to Goldmarket Square where the bikers wandered around, gazing up into the ancient Exceptional Tree and at the shops that lined the Square. The Sweet Potato had its sign turned to 'open' from when she'd burst out into the rain, but Franco's Patisserie was closed firmly for his

Christmas holiday. Further back, the old bank that was Roman and Jules's The Leftover Restaurant had its doors firmly closed even though its chef and his wife were in Mulbury for Christmas. Kelly's Mullings of Mulbury was lit cheerfully from within, with Kelly herself watching the action through her window, arms crossed. Rosemary ignored her and went to the grey-bearded man standing next to Rakisha waiting patiently for her to notice him. Despite him towering over the woman, Rakisha started to wave her arms and bounce around with her eyes closed. Rosemary coughed politely. 'Perhaps I can help you?'

The grey-bearded man startled. 'Yeah, right, sorry. I was just going to ask this lady whether there's somewhere we could shelter for a time but she's...well...'

'Dancing?'

'I guess that's what she's doing.'

Rakisha lowered her arms and stared at the man for the first time. 'I am taking in the goodness that the earth mother provides for us.'

The man blinked and nodded slowly as the rain started its heavy pace again. 'That's, yep, great.'

'You're looking for a place to put your bikes?' asked Rosemary.

The man tore his gaze from Rakisha and looked at Rosemary. 'The bikes are okay. We're worried about the presents.' He waved his arms at the receptacles on the motorcycles. 'These are usually great at keeping the water out but this rain is not what we'd call *usual*. We're gonna stop for an hour or two.'

Rosemary eyed the panniers. 'What about parking your bikes under the veranda? That would keep them drier.'

The man looked across at where Mrs Lionel, Jasper,

Patti and Gerry stood. 'Hey, yeah, that would be great.' He waved a finger at the sidecars. 'We'd better check these sacks. Not as watertight as the panniers. Anywhere we could unpack them that's dry?'

'The veranda might not be the best to unload a stack of presents.'

'What about my café?'

Rosemary turned at the high-pitched voice. Kelly Flanagan stood in the teeming rain, sheltering under a large pink umbrella. She extended it so that it half covered the grey-bearded man but not Rosemary.

'Sorry, lady. What *about* your café?'

'You could put your sacks in there and sort the presents out on the tables.' Kelly indicated the café behind her, her dark bobbed hair swaying as she turned. 'I'm not expecting any customers soon and, besides, you'd be quite a drawcard if people did turn up.' She widened her eyes. 'Cracker Christmas Kids is a well-known charity and you're all such *interesting* looking men.'

Rosemary glanced around at the riders shrugging their jackets up around their ears to stop the rain pouring down their necks. Interesting the bearded men were, although the way Kelly said it was just short of sarcastic.

'Well, thanks...'

'Kelly.'

'Thanks, Kelly.' The man held out an enormous hand to shake hers. 'I'm Tommy.'

'Pleased to meet you, Tommy.' Kelly let his hand go and pointed. 'This way.'

'I'll just sort these fellas out.' Tommy went back to his friends.

Rosemary watched as Tommy shifted his bike to under

the veranda, heaved the sack from the sidecar, and walked back, dodging some wayward bikes as they drove up the gutter. She wiped the rain from her face. 'Magnanimous of you, Kelly Flanagan.'

'Well, they aren't the only ones with a bit of Christmas spirit.' Kelly tipped the umbrella so it covered the back of her head more readily. She beckoned to Tommy as he approached. 'Besides, they'll probably buy lunch. I've got a living to make, you know.'

'Yes. Your Christmas spirit extends only so far.'

'Now, now, Rosemary Exeter.' Kelly started back to her café, followed by Tommy and an equally burly man with tufty grey mutton chops accompanying his beard who were bent over with the weight of the sacks on their backs. 'Maybe they'll want some jars of jam later and I bet you won't be giving them away.' She turned back to the men. 'My, aren't you strong! Those sacks look ridiculously heavy.'

'They are,' said Tommy.

'Yeah,' panted the other man, making his slow way up the few steps that led into the cafe. 'Heavier than I remember...' His voice disappeared as he put his effort into carrying.

Rosemary followed the men with the sacks to allow the motorcycles room to manoeuvre over to the veranda. Kelly held the door open for them, letting it go as Rosemary got to it, effectively shutting her out. Rosemary got the hint and instead watched the moving parade in front of her from the partial shelter of the café's eave. The remaining bikers rumbled slowly over to the veranda, and the noise hid what was happening in café. As the machines switched off, a shriek rang out inside Mullings.

As Rosemary turned, she glimpsed what had caused

Kelly's shout. The sacks lay open on the floor, but instead of only a variety of coloured parcels spilling across the floorboards, a hairy arm poked out of each and lay lifeless among the Christmas presents.

# TWO

Rosemary wrenched the café door open and stepped inside, sliding momentarily on the wet floor and coming to rest against Tommy. The man stood stiffly, his mouth open, and his eyes bulging. The one with the mutton chops crouched groaning on the floor, tugging the sacks away from the bodies within.

Kelly backed away until she hit a table. 'Oh, gosh, are they dead?'

Rosemary knelt and tried to find a pulse in the first arm. Nothing. The skin was cold and pale despite its glossy covering of coarse ginger hair. She went to the next one and felt nothing there either. It, too, was covered in ginger hair. If the two sacks, and therefore what they contained, had been closer on the floor, it would be easy to assume the arms belonged to the same person. Instead, the open sacks revealed two gentlemen, both with glorious red beards, dressed in matching dapper tweed waistcoats and navy trousers.

'Ted,' whispered Tommy. 'Ned.'

'That's what their names were?' asked Rosemary. 'Twins?'

'Yes.' Tommy's voice had lowered even further. 'Ted and Ned 'O'Reilly. The only twins in our band of brothers.' He staggered back and half-fell into a chair. 'They weren't even expected to be here this weekend.'

Rosemary looked at Kelly but she had retreated further. She stood against the shop counter, talking on the phone. 'I'm calling the police,' she said to Rosemary's raised eyebrows. 'Something you should have thought of.'

'As if I hadn't,' muttered Rosemary, settling down on her heels to look more closely at the first prostrate brother. 'Is this Ned?'

'That's Ted,' said mutton chops, pointing at a faint birthmark on the dead man's cheek. 'Ned doesn't have that.'

Rosemary studied what she could see of Ted. Having been unceremoniously dumped out of his sack, he sprawled on the café floor untidily, arms and legs at unusual angles. The waistcoat buttoned neatly and sat on his hips, while the heavy black boots he wore shone dully with new polish. She glanced across at Ned, and he presented similarly, although his boots were tan and his cheeks free of pigmentation. Both had their eyes three quarters closed, revealing sky blue pupils. Faint white dried scum settled at the corners of Ted's mouth.

She sat back. 'What do you mean, they weren't expected to be here this weekend?'

'Well, just that.' Tommy wiped at his face. 'They had to go to a city lawyer about their mother's will. Their father's been dead for decades but their mother died a few months' ago. It's taken a while to sort out her estate. She had a *lot* of assets. Rich as blazes, by all accounts.'

'Anyway,' said mutton chops. 'They'd done a lot of work

collecting presents last weekend.' He lifted his chin towards the row of motorbikes under the veranda. 'The sacks fit in their sidecars pretty good.'

'The motorcycles with the sidecars belonged to them?'

'Yeah.' Mutton chops scratched his hairy chin. 'But they'd loaned them to Harry, hadn't they, Tommy?'

'Yep,' said Tommy, taking a shuddering breath in and out. 'Harry and Gordy.' He rubbed his face. 'We'll have to tell them about...' He waved at the bodies on the floor. 'And Bill and Rock.'

'Will they be upset?' asked Rosemary, standing up.

'Oh, for heavens' sake,' said Kelly, coming forward so she stood at Tommy's chair. 'Of course, they'll be upset! Their friends are dead.'

Tommy glanced at mutton chops. 'Well...'

Rosemary gave him a sharp look. 'Well what? They weren't your friends?'

'It's hard to explain.' He waved his hand again, this time at mutton chops. 'Moose, you try.'

Moose grimaced. 'It's not that they were bad blokes, it's just that they weren't very friendly.'

'So, we don't really think of them as friends.'

'No, not friends. Fellow charity riders?'

Kelly frowned. 'But you did know them?' She raised her voice over the increasing volume of rain outside. 'I mean, they weren't complete strangers?'

'No,' bellowed Tommy, as thunder boomed over the café. 'Not strangers but we don't know a lot about them personally.'

'You knew about their mother,' yelled Rosemary as torrents flowed down the windows, blocking the Square from view.

'Yeah, but everyone knew that's why they weren't going to be here this weekend.'

Lightning flashed overhead, brightening the room for a split second, followed by a massive thunder crack. The café went dark.

'Power gone,' said Moose into the gloom.

'No kidding, Einstein.' Tommy stared down at Ned and Ted. 'No power, tonnes of rain. Do you reckon the police will get through?'

Rosemary pulled out her phone and connected to her weather app. Flood warnings flashed all over it. 'The road to Big Town is closed.'

'Can they come from any other direction?'

'It'll take them hours.'

'So, we're stuck with...' Kelly nodded towards the twins. 'Great. Will they go off in this heat, do you think?'

Rosemary was used to people scowling at her bluntness so it was a nice change that Tommy and Moose directed their horror at the café owner instead. Tommy covered his mouth as if he was going to be sick. Rosemary turned quickly. 'How about we cover them up? Kelly, have you got any large tablecloths?'

Kelly nodded and went into the back of her shop to fetch them, leaving Moose standing with drooped shoulders beside Ted and Tommy leaning forward, elbows on thighs, towards Ned.

Rosemary squatted again to study the brothers. Moose had pulled the sacks completely off the bodies, spilling more than human beings out on the floor. Both sacks contained several presents in the same green wrapping paper. A couple of rectangular packages lay next to Ned, one with its corner ripped. She took photos of the scene, then reached for the ripped parcel.

'What are you doing?' said Tommy in alarm.

'These are all donated presents?'

'Yeah. We've been collecting them for a month.'

'New presents? No second-hand things?'

'No, all new. If people can't give us presents they've bought for the kiddies, they donate money so we can buy stuff.'

Rosemary lifted the present up so Tommy could see. 'This one isn't new.'

She didn't blame Tommy for peering closely at the present in the gloom, but it took longer than necessary for him to react to what she had seen. 'Wait on', she said. She unstuck the ripped wrapping paper and tipped a book out of a cardboard box.

Another lightning flash lit the room and, for a moment, the dog-eared book was clearly visible. It was a hardback, stiff also with age. 'The Comedy of Errors by William Shakespeare,' read Kelly, coming back to the bodies clutching two tablecloths. 'Who would donate a second-hand Shakespeare?'

'Maybe it was an accident,' said Rosemary. 'Perhaps someone wrapped it up by mistake.'

'Or maybe it's a really good story.' Kelly fluffed out the cloths and settled them over the dead men. 'Someone's book from when they were a kid and they wanted to share it.'

Rosemary opened it and turned the page so Tommy could see. 'You mean, someone with a name starting with T wanted to share it.'

The grey-bearded man stared at the writing Rosemary had her finger against. 'To my darling T, from Mummy.' He chewed his lip for a moment then brightened. 'T for Ted!'

Rosemary shrugged.

Tommy looked at Moose and shook his head. 'I don't get

it how Ted and Ned could be in those sacks. We packed them.'

Thunder rolled again, a little further away. The rain eased, too. Rosemary could once again see out the window to the huddle of bikes across Goldmarket Road. Moose raised his head. 'I'll go and tell them.'

Tommy put his head in his hands. 'What are you going to say, Moose?'

Moose chewed his lip for a moment, making his sideburns wriggle. 'I'm going to tell them the truth.'

'What truth?'

'Oh, come on, Tommy.' Moose nudged the closest sack with his toe. 'You don't think Ted and Ned climbed into these by themselves?'

'They did last night when they hid in the sacks and jumped out, scaring the life out of us.'

'Tommy, it's obvious, isn't it? They've been *murdered*!'

The last word was partly covered by a dramatic growl from the sky, but it only served to make it more chilling. Kelly squealed quietly and Tommy sucked in his breath. 'No, Moose. No.'

'You got any other explanation?'

Tommy separated his fingers just enough to see the bodies in front of him. 'None. It just doesn't make sense. Who'd wanna do that?'

'We don't know, do we?' Moose headed to the door. 'Maybe Ted and Ned knew something they shouldn't have.' He wrenched the door open and went out into the rain.

Rosemary stood up again and glanced at her watch. It would be hours before the police got to them. She went to one of the café tables and sat down to flick through the ragged book. Apart from its gift dedication, the pages were unmarked although the whole book showed signs of endless reading. Some pages were worn so badly, the words had faded, and the spine cracked in several places as if pushed flat too many times by a reader. She peered at Ted again, seeing the outline of spectacles in his top pocket. But then Ned had them, too, as would most gentlemen of their age.

Tommy stood suddenly, his chair tipping and crashing onto the floor. 'Sorry,' he said. 'I can't stand being in here any longer.' He ran for the door and crashed out.

'I feel the same,' said Kelly, waving a hand at the bodies while keeping her face averted. 'It's so morbid. I'm going.' She turned to Rosemary. 'Of course, you'll stay. Your dark tendencies will keep you here.'

'Not dark,' said Rosemary, although Kelly had already gone out the back door. 'Just curious.'

The noise of the rain had quietened substantially, leaving the café eerily silent. The rain may have abated but the clouds were even thicker, and the gloom deepened. Rosemary stared at the men on the floor and decided. She crouched down, shucked off the tablecloths, pulled the sleeve of her coat over her fingers, and fished around in the men's pockets for anything that may shine a skerrick of light on why he'd ended up in a sack.

Ned's back trouser pocket contained a slim wallet, a clean handkerchief that smelled like washing powder, and a pill container. The spectacles were the only thing in his waistcoat, but he had half a bottle of orange juice in his front trouser pocket. She moved to Ted. His pockets held a wallet, a rumpled hanky that smelled a bit like a dry-cleaning shop, and a pill container. Ned's wallet held one twenty-dollar note, a driver's licence and a coffee loyalty card. Ted's held one twenty-dollar note, a licence, and a coffee loyalty card for a different café. Rosemary spread the contents out on the floor. Nothing out of the ordinary there, although the contents were eerily similar.

A rap at the door made her look up. Jasper Lu pushed his way in, his long dark hair flying around in the wind and settling across his shoulders as he shut the door. 'You alright?' he asked. 'I mean, you're babysitting...' He glanced at the floor and shuddered.

'Corpse-sitting, actually.' Rosemary pointed to the table where she'd sat to read the book. 'What do you make of that?'

Jasper walked gingerly over to the table and picked up the book. Rosemary let him ponder, leaning over the items on the floor to study them more closely.

'One of Shakespeare's comedies,' said Jasper eventually. 'Although I prefer Twelfth Night. I've got a lot of copies in my shop so it's been on a school reading list before.' He turned the book over. 'This copy is much older than what I have. Why do you have it?'

But Rosemary didn't answer. Instead, she beckoned Jasper over and pulled at his hand to make him squat.

'Rosemary,' he said, his face pale. 'I don't really like...'

'Shhh, Jasper,' she said, tugging him down so that he was over the objects on the floor. 'Tell me what you see.'

'Do these things belong to those men? Rosemary, you shouldn't have touched...'

'Quiet, Jasper. Just look.'

Jasper chewed his lip but stared obediently at the floor. 'I can't see anything-'

'Look.' Rosemary tapped one of the licences. 'See the name?'

'Timothy Armstrong. So?'

Rosemary sat back. 'So, there is no Timothy Armstrong in this room.'

# THREE

From the blank look on Jasper's face, Rosemary could see he didn't get it. She shook her finger at Ned's wallet. 'The licence was in there. Why would Ned O'Reilly have a licence belonging to a Timothy Armstrong?'

'He was minding it for a friend?'

Rosemary shook her head at Jasper. 'Perhaps.'

'We could ask them.' Jasper indicated the row of motor-cycles gathered under the veranda opposite. 'Maybe they know who Timothy is. Perhaps he's part of their group. I'll go.' He backed away from the men on the floor and almost ran out of the door.

Rosemary spent a moment longer studying Ted and Ned, but their bodies remained silent and she left the café without any further clues. The bikers were grouped outside Patricia's as Patti served them cold drinks while Jasper chatted to them. Mrs Lionel and Gerry stood with their arms around Rakisha outside The Preserved Mulbury. 'Goodness,' said Mrs Lionel, rubbing Rakisha's back firmly. 'What a turn of events right before Christmas.'

'Quite a shock,' said Gerry. 'Some of us are taking it worse than others.' He tipped his head towards Rakisha.

'Oh, darling,' said Rakisha, looking up at Rosemary with watery eyes. 'Are they alright? The men?'

Rosemary studied the woman in front of her. Rakisha's long grey spiralled hair was drenched and lengthened nearly to her waist, tangling in the various layers of fabric draping her thin body. 'They're dead, Rakisha.'

'Well, yes, I know that.' Rakisha flapped her hand dismissively. 'I mean, did they appear at peace with the universe? Were their souls resting?'

'A bit hard to tell because they were-'

'Right,' said Mrs Lionel, her free hand now on Rosemary's arm. 'How about we help Patti with the remainder of the charitable group? I think they could do with some sustenance. We could make sandwiches.'

'Bring them into my shop,' said Rosemary. 'I baked bread yesterday.'

Rosemary left Mrs Lionel to steer Rakisha into The Preserved Mulbury and went to get the biker brothers and Jasper. 'Any reaction to Timothy Armstrong's name?' she whispered to him as walked to The Preserved Mulbury's door.

'Blank stares.'

'From everyone?'

'Well, Rosemary, it's a bit hard to look at six people at once.' He bent down and scooped up a letter that had been on the floor and handed it to Rosemary as she came back. 'Christmas greetings, probably.'

Rosemary stuffed the letter into her jacket pocket, earning a stern look from Mrs Lionel over Rakisha's shoulder. 'Be a bit careful with it, dear,' the older woman whispered. 'I know who it's from.'

Rosemary said nothing.

The bikers left their jackets and helmets on their motor-bikes and drifted inside Rosemary's shop talking quietly. Sunny took one look at the entourage and leapt down from her lounge room windowsill, giving Rosemary a look that said, *You have got to be joking*.

Rosemary ran her hand down Sunny's smooth, ginger-striped coat. 'Sorry, Sunny. You'll have to be a tolerant cat until the rain goes.'

*Tolerance,* the tabby seemed to say as she stalked to Rosemary's bedroom, *is not my thing*.

The electricity was still off so Rosemary served iced tea and cheese and pickle sandwiches which were devoured by the bikers, leaving only the crusts for the Mulburians. 'Thank you,' said one dark-haired man. 'This is very good of you.'

'It's not a problem,' said Rosemary, offering him another sandwich.

'We missed breakfast, didn't we, Gordy?' The man poked his brother.

Gordy nodded. 'We were rushing to get ready, eh, Harry?' He nudged his brother. 'We probably rushed too much.'

A white-haired biker gave a short chuckle. 'You're always rushing, you two. Lucky for you the sacks were already in the sidecars before you got to them.' He sobered. 'Well, I think it was lucky. Who put them in there in the first place?'

Gordy glanced at Harry. 'Don't know, Bill. That's how we found them when we arrived this morning.'

'Must have been Tommy,' said the other white-haired man.

'Or Moose,' said Bill.

'Or both of them,' said Harry. 'They're the strongest of us.'

Gordy shovelled another sandwich in his mouth and took a moment to swallow. 'We were all in a rush yesterday and again this morning. I reckon I packed and repacked those panniers ten times to fit everything in. That made me late.'

'Yeah,' Rock said. 'It was busy alright. Come to think of it, it could have been Ned and Ted who put the sacks in the sidecars last night. They were there to pack, although they both looked a bit under the weather. Ted kept drinking that orange concoction Ned gave him, and Ted kept offering Ned a hanky.'

Gordy gave a short laugh. 'Strong little fellows, though, weren't they? I could easily see them putting loaded sacks in, sick or not.'

'Little being the word. About half my size.' Rock patted his abdomen.

'Well,' said his brother. 'We don't call you Rock for nothing. Ted and Ned were more like pebbles compared to you.'

'Yeah, well, they scared me half to death when they hid in those sacks and jumped out, pebbles or not.'

'Ha, yeah, they like playing that stupid game. They did it last night to me.'

'And me.'

At the way they were scowling, Rosemary could see that Ted and Ned's game hadn't been funny to anyone else but them. She offered the last sandwich to the men and went back to see what bread was left. Jasper was happily spreading his crust thickly with the previous season's jumbleberry jam, while Rakisha mixed the pickles with the jam and ate the bread end heartedly without noticing the astonishment on Jasper's face.

'I wonder when the police will get here,' said Mrs Lionel. She glanced out the window. 'This weather won't help.'

It was raining heavily again, thick sheets of it plastering Rosemary's glass door that led out to her porch. It made it steamy inside, and the bikers started shedding their shirts, leaving many of them in blue worker's singlets. Mrs Lionel moved to stand under the ceiling fan in Rosemary's living area, while Rosemary gathered plates to take to her kitchen. Jasper swept his glass up and followed her. 'Those beards must be hot,' he said quietly to Rosemary. 'Not really the current climate for them.'

'Maybe beards act like the coats on huskies,' said Rosemary. 'Insulating the skin.' She glanced down. 'Jasper, did you take that book with you?'

Jasper swallowed the last of his bread and felt his back pocket. 'Oh, whoops.' He pulled the Shakespeare out. 'It's evidence, of a kind. I should give it to the police.'

Rosemary shrugged. 'They'll be a long time yet.'

'You know,' Jasper said, turning the book over in his hands. 'Shakespeare wrote a lot about siblings.'

Rosemary tapped the book in his hand. 'Remind me who features in this one?'

'Brothers.' He hmphed. 'Twins to be exact.'

Thunder rolled, promising a heightened storm, and its sound nearly covered the protesting jangling of the door as someone else pushed inside. Rosemary went back into her shop to find Jules Capriccio looking unusually unkempt dripping water onto the floorboards. 'My apology, Rosemary,' Jules said, folding her hair behind her ears. 'I didn't mean to make such an entrance.'

'Are you okay, Jules?' Jasper said. 'You look...'

'Saturated,' finished Rosemary. 'Would you like a towel?'

'That would be lovely but first I must ask whether you've seen Roman?'

Rosemary frowned. Roman Capriccio was not a man to disappear on his wife. He could usually be found in the kitchen of his restaurant or his home, inventing delicious dinners and desserts. 'Perhaps he's out buying ingredients from Justin and got caught in the weather?'

'I've rung Justin at the farm.' Jules shrugged. 'Roman was there but he left a while ago.'

'Did Roman buy anything?'

'Vegetables.' Jules sighed. 'It's been hours. And then the rain started.'

'That'll be it,' said Jasper. 'He'll be sheltering some-where until it stops.'

Rosemary left Jules with Jasper and went to fetch towels. The pairs of bikers nodded their thanks for lunch at her as she passed, and she noted how sombre they looked. Now that she had a chance to discriminate between them, she saw that there were three pairs: the grey-haired Tommy and Moose; Bill and Rock with matching white plaited beards; and the younger dark-haired Harry and Gordy who stood away from the others speaking quietly to each other.

Jules took the towel gratefully and carefully squeezed the rain from her hair. She patted her cheeks dry and spent a moment too long with the towel over her eyes.

'What is it, Jules?' asked Rosemary. 'What's really both-ering you?'

Jules lowered the towel and Rosemary glimpsed the red of her eyes before Jules looked away. 'It's Roman,' she said. 'He's not himself.'

'What do you mean?' asked Jasper. 'I saw him yesterday when he came into The Read Mulbury. He seems okay.'

'He probably does to you.' Jules sighed. 'The last few weeks, though, he hasn't been his usual self.' She let the towel dangle from her hands. 'He burned an apple pie.'

Rosemary felt Mrs Lionel's hand on her arm before she could answer. She turned to see her best friend looking with concern at Jules. 'He burned a pie, dear?'

'Yes.'

'I imagine he hasn't burned a pie since he was in culinary school.'

'Exactly, Mrs Lionel.' Jules folded the towel in half and took a second one from Rosemary to drape around her shoulders. 'Not only that, but the custard was lumpy.'

Rosemary felt the grip on her arm tighten but she couldn't help herself. 'Lumpy custard is just terrible.'

Jules gave her a sharp look. 'It is, Rosemary, when it comes to my husband. You know that.'

'Sorry, Jules.' Rosemary thought of the cheerful Roman whose walrus moustache often hid a smile. 'You're right. It doesn't sound like Roman.'

'I could recite a list of odd small things that have gone wrong in the kitchen over the last little while, none of which have ended in complete disaster until the pie. That happened last night.'

'How did he react, dear? To the burnt pie?'

'Well, he reacted strangely. He threw it in the bin.'

That shocked Rosemary much more than the burning. Roman and Jules ran The Leftover Restaurant and prided themselves on using every bit of produce given to them. If it couldn't be eaten by humans, it was often given to Justin for the various animals on his farm. The chickens would have loved an apple pie, burnt or not.

Jasper looked at Rosemary in concern. 'Would you like me to go to Big Town, Jules, and see if I can find him?'

'That seems silly, doesn't it?' Jules played with the edge of the towel. 'I mean, look at it.'

They turned as one to gaze out the window where rain swept sideways in a vicious wind.

'I hope the creek isn't flooding.' Jules flicked a strand of hair away from her face with one delicate finger. 'Everyone will be stuck here if it is.'

'It wasn't,' said Mrs Lionel, indicating the Bearded Biker Brothers. 'But it might be now. The road was flooded and if the creek is up, there'll be a whole stretch under water.'

Jules startled as if just noticing the mob of bikers milling around Rosemary's lounge and shop. 'Oh, have I interrupted a party?'

'A wake, more likely.' Rosemary quickly explained the situation. 'The police have been notified.'

'Goodness, what a dreadful incident.' Jules checked her hair with a trembling hand. 'Any idea of what happened?'

'None at all,' said Jasper.

Jules nodded towards Tommy and Moose. 'Are they the leaders of the group? I could ask them if they've seen Roman on their way to Mulbury?'

'That's a good idea.' Mrs Lionel looped her arm through Jules's. 'Let's ask.'

Jasper shook his head as the women left. 'I don't know, Rosemary. It does sound strange for Roman to disappear without telling Jules.'

'It does.' Rosemary eyed the bikers who'd been whispering to each other near the linen closet as they helped himself to another sandwich. 'We've got a few things to watch out for.'

'Like what?'

'I'm not sure yet but don't you think it strange that two dead men have been travelling around in sidecars all day without anyone noticing?'

'The Brothers were taking the presents to a delivery centre. They thought the sacks were full.'

'Full indeed.'

'Rosemary,' said Jasper. 'Do you think the murderer is in this room?'

Rosemary took in the bearded men in her living room. They still stood in pairs, brushing breadcrumbs from their hairy chins and talking quietly. None were particularly upset, although they looked serious.

The lights flickered and came on strongly, making the crowd cheer briefly. Now that the men were illuminated, Rosemary saw two had bits of green wrapping paper and ribbon protruding from their pockets, as if they'd hastily finished covering the presents before they'd got on their bikes. She nudged Jasper. 'See?'

Jasper peered at where she was looking. 'No?'

'The paper in Tommy and Moose's pockets.' She nodded towards the men sipping cups of tea. 'It's the same paper that was used for the presents in the sacks.'

'So?'

'How did they put the presents in the sack without noticing the twins were in there as well?'

Jasper chewed his lip for a moment. 'Maybe they did notice?'

Rosemary narrowed her eyes at the grey-haired men. 'Precisely.'

# FOUR

The day wore on, intermittently dark with storms. Kelly stood in The Preserved Mulbury, her nose close to the window, gazing out to her shop. Rosemary offered her a cup of tea and she shook her head violently. 'No offence, Rosemary Exeter, but your tea is always too strong.'

'No offence taken,' said Rosemary, meaning it. If strong tea kept Kelly away from her, then she'd add extra leaves to the pot.

'Now then, Rosemary.' Mrs Lionel joined her back in the kitchen as another round of sandwiches, this time from defrosted bread, went out to the bearded men. 'I saw you with Kelly.'

'I offered her tea.'

'That was very nice of you.'

'She refused.'

'*Refusal* is a harsh word. She declined, more like it.'

Rosemary turned to her friend. 'If you offered, I bet she'd have a cup.'

Mrs Lionel smiled. 'Of course, she would. I'd make it to her liking.'

'You are too good.'

'I'm not, you know. I'm more flexible than you, however.'

Rosemary tossed her long braid back over her shoulder. 'I can be flexible when I want to be.'

'Which means you aren't very often.' Mrs Lionel picked up a tea towel and started to dry the teacups in the drainer. 'When are you going to let the misunderstanding between Kelly and you go?'

'*Misunderstanding?*'

Mrs Lionel paused her drying. 'Don't get all haughty with me, dear. Yes, *misunderstanding* is what I called it.'

'She flirted with my husband.'

'Alasdair was a handsome man.' Mrs Lionel shrugged. 'I flirted with him myself.'

'Yes, but...' Rosemary exhaled loudly.

'But a woman in her eighties wasn't a threat, was I? Kelly Flanagan hurt your pride.'

Rosemary held Mrs Lionel's blue-eyed gaze. Her friend wore her usual kindly expression but there was a slight twinkle apparent. 'It was bad timing. It was just before he disappeared.'

Any trace of mirth left Mrs Lionel's face. 'I know. That was a horrible time in your life.'

'I thought...'

'What, dear?'

Rosemary pulled herself straight. 'I thought he'd gone off with her.'

'Ah.' Mrs Lionel nodded slowly. 'I see.'

'But he hadn't.'

'No, he hadn't. So, it might be time to forgive Kelly.'

'I have.' Rosemary opened the tin on the bench and

pulled out a Christmas cake. 'That doesn't mean I have to like her.'

Before she could slice the cake, Kelly hurried over brandishing her phone. 'The police. They're delayed. Probably until tomorrow.'

'I thought they would be, dear.' Mrs Lionel took the knife from Rosemary's clenched fist. 'Anything that we should do?'

'They didn't say.' She tapped the phone on her chin, staring down at Rosemary's cake. 'I should fetch some of my slices.'

Rosemary moved away from Mrs Lionel's nudge. 'To sell to these men?'

'The police aren't the only ones who've been delayed.' Kelly waved the phone around. 'They'll be stuck here just as long and maybe they'd like to take slices with them when they go. For Christmas.' She tucked a strand of hair behind her ear. 'I have gift boxes.'

'They're on motorbikes.'

'So? They have their panniers.'

'Full of presents.'

'Well, anyway, I'm sure they'd cope.' Kelly slid her phone into her jeans pocket. 'I should fetch some...'

'But there are two dead bodies on your café.'

Kelly glared at Rosemary. 'I gave permission for the sacks to be in my café. Not the bodies.'

'But there they are.'

'Now, dear,' said Mrs Lionel, a hand on Rosemary's forearm. 'I'm sure Rosemary would get the slices for you. To share, mind. Not to sell. These poor bikers have had enough to deal with today.'

Kelly frowned, then tossed her head so her bob swung

like a pendulum. 'A sample of my slices would be just the thing. Better than...' She pointed a finger at the Christmas cake.

'Rosemary's cake is delicious,' said Mrs Lionel firmly. 'But a range of slices would be lovely.' She glanced outside at the dull day. 'Especially if our guests are around for a while. And look. The rain has stopped for a moment.'

As Rosemary glanced outside, the sun forced its way through the clouds and blazed down. Jasper opened the wide glass door to the balcony, letting in much-needed fresh air, and some of the bearded brothers filtered outside.

'Alright,' said Rosemary. 'I'll get your slices. Not your gift boxes.'

Kelly smiled. 'Why, thank you, Rosemary. How very kind.'

'Hmph.' Rosemary left the kitchen and retrieved an umbrella from her laundry. Tommy and Moose tipped their heads at her as she went past. She stopped. 'Excuse me,' she said. 'Would you mind helping me get some cakes from Kelly's café?'

At first, she thought they were going to refuse, but Tommy glanced at Moose. 'The café? Where the sacks are? And Ted and Ned?'

'Yes.' She tipped her head to one side. 'Does that stress you? I could ask the others.'

Tommy considered her request, chewing the inside of his cheek and making his beard bob up and down. 'No. We can do it. Better us than any of the others. We've already seen them.'

'Take this, then.' Rosemary thrust a tray at him. 'I'll bring another.'

Tommy and Moose followed her obediently as she went through The Preserved Mulbury and stepped outside. The

Exceptional Tree, its gigantic trunk grey from the rain, waved its ancient branches at her as Rosemary wove her way through the puddles in Goldmarket Square to Mullings of Mulbury. Clouds once again greyed the sun, and thunder rolled. 'Will it ever stop?' murmured Moose behind her.

They halted at the door of Mullings. The inside light was cheery but the sprawled men on the floor looked too pale. Rosemary wrenched the door open and held it for the burly men behind her who stepped in gingerly.

'Yikes,' said Moose.

'Crikey,' said Tommy.

Rosemary stepped over the spilled presents and went behind Kelly's counter to start loading slices into cardboard trays. She kept one eye on the men, who were now standing shoulder to shoulder talking quietly. Now that they were together, she saw that Moose was taller than Tommy by half a head but that their physiques were similar. Both men were built like brick outhouses and she understood how easily they could heft the sacks plus the twins from the sidecars. She put down the cake slide she was using to shimmy jelly slice across and went to them. 'Are you alright?'

Tommy nodded his head and Moose shook his.

Rosemary tried to channel Rakisha. 'They look peaceful.'

'They look dead,' said Moose.

'That, too.'

'Do you think we'll be able to get to those soon?' asked Tommy.

'Get to what?'

He nodded towards the scattered pile of presents. 'Those.'

'The police will need to look at them, I'm guessing.'

Tommy glanced at Moose and shook his head. 'They may not make it for Christmas, then.'

'No.'

Tommy's fists clenched by his side.

Rosemary stuffed more slices into her tray. 'Maybe we could buy some more so you don't need those ones. Do you know what's in them?'

'Oh, yeah. I do the selection and distribution of those presents.'

'Selection?'

'You know, trying to guess what age group each one is suitable for.' He let his fists relax.

'And you organise their wrapping before distribution.'

Tommy's eyebrows disappeared into his fringe. 'How did you know that?'

'You have wrapping paper in your back pocket.'

Tommy moved to feel his pocket. 'Do I? What colour is it?'

'Green.'

'Oh. Well. There you have it.'

Rosemary waited but Tommy said nothing. She sighed. 'What sorts of presents are they? So, we can see if we can buy replacements.'

'You won't be able to,' said Moose. 'Not at short notice.'

'Why not?'

Moose waved his hand at the presents. 'They're electronic gadgets. Tablets and laptop computers mainly.'

'Not all of them.'

Tommy paled. 'No. That's right. The book.'

Rosemary thought of the book she'd found. It had been in a flat box and, wrapped, could easily have been mistaken for something else. 'Computers must have been expensive for the donors.'

'The people we ask directly for donations can afford it.'

'The people of Mulbury won't be able to.' She stared at Moose. 'Did you two put the sacks into the sidecars?'

'Us? Well, yeah.' Moose glanced at Tommy. 'We loaded the sacks this morning before the others got there.'

'Yeah,' said Tommy. 'We were early so we grabbed them, tied the tops, and threw them in.'

'Don't you think it strange you didn't notice two men in there as well as presents?'

Tommy paused. 'We thought we knew what was in there. And it wasn't bodies.'

Rosemary waited but Tommy was looking out the window at the rain as if it was a new phenomenon and didn't say anything more.

Moose shuffled his feet. 'Time to go?'

His brother nodded.

Rosemary collected a tray of slices and went out the door Moose was holding open. The rain was belting down again, making swirly rivers of the Square. She ducked her head and made a run for it, the big men lumbering after her. With her head down to avoid the deluge, Rosemary almost ran into Patti and Gerry standing watch.

Patti jumped back and laughed. 'Oops, Rosemary! Nearly got me.'

'Watch those cakes,' Gerry said.

Rosemary steadied them. 'Got them.'

'Oh, Kelly's slices!' said Patti. 'What a shame. We were just heading off.'

Rosemary studied the teeming rain and then the pair in front of her. 'In this?'

'We promised Jules we'd look for Roman,' said Gerry, his round face wrinkling in concern. 'She hasn't located him.'

'Where is she now?'

'She went back home in case he'd gone there and missed her.'

'Where are you going to look?'

'We'll do a drive-by of the farm and then head towards Big Town as far as we can go until the flood waters stop us.' Gerry slipped his hand into Patti's. 'I'm sure Roman will be okay. Perhaps the weather is affecting his phone reception.'

'I hope you're right, Gerry.' Patti twirled a wave of rose-gold hair that curled at her neck. 'Such a worry for Jules.'

'We'll see you shortly, Rosemary.' Gerry lifted his hand, dragging Patti's along with it, to indicate Mullings of Mulbury. 'I hope they solve that before too long.'

Rosemary watched as the pair walked back along the pavement and separated to manoeuvre around the motor-bikes still parked under cover. As they disappeared around the corner to go to their car, the big men pushed their way back into The Preserved Mulbury but Rosemary hesitated. 'Here,' she called after Moose. 'Take these in and I'll be there shortly.'

He took the tray. 'Okay, then?'

'No.' Rosemary tipped her head at him. 'We have two dead men in a café, and another man missing in dreadful weather. What would be alright about that?'

Under the expanse of hair covering his face, Moose's skin went scarlet. He lifted the slices in acknowledgement and disappeared inside.

Rosemary smoothed the dampness from her face and went to inspect the bikes. They had club plates, meaning they were only ridden for special occasions. Perhaps only for the Cracker Christmas Kids Charity collection and distribution. She squatted beside a sidecar, admiring the carefully stencilled striping on its side. These were no ordinary motorbikes, but well-kept and tended. Except for...

She reached down into the shell of the sidecar, poking under its nose, and pulled out a tatty book. She opened it. Inside the cover, in clear blue copperplate, writing read: *To my darling Tommy, from Mummy.*

# FIVE

Mrs Lionel left The Preserved Mulbury shortly after Rosemary had exited to get Kelly's cakes and went back to her home for a rest. As she opened the door to The Green Mulbury, the frog-shaped electronic motion sensor went into a frenzy. She shut the door quickly and moved out of its range, making silence fall in the shop. The sweet fragrance of drying herbs, rose-scented soaps and eucalyptus-tinted laundry liquid felt calming and she sighed contentedly. 'What a haven to enter, Percy,' she said to the ghostly fox terrier wagging his tail at her from the doorway to her living quarters.

Outside, on the adjoining balcony, the murmur of men's voices reminded her of The Bearded Biker Brothers and their ill-fated journey. She went to the linen press in the corner of the lounge room and opened its broad double doors to search for hidden gifts. The cupboard had been a storage place for plum puddings, boxes of hankies, and random purchases intended for someone's birthday. *Perhaps,* she thought, *I might have some things suitable for Cracker Christmas children.*

With her head deep in the cupboard, it wasn't until Percy gave a menacing growl that she realised she wasn't alone. She stepped back and slammed the door shut, revealing a startled man with a black beard. 'What are you doing?' she said loudly.

The man backed away with his hands in the air. 'So sorry, lady,' he said, clearly unable to hear Percy's ethereal barking. 'I didn't mean to scare you.'

'I am not scared,' said Mrs Lionel, shushing Percy with a wave of her hand. 'Merely curious as to why you're in my living room. It's Harry, isn't it?'

'Yeah.' The man glanced around, as if he'd just noticed where he was. 'I'm sorry, I don't think I realised. I just needed to get away.' He gestured outside to the balcony with its waist high railing. 'I climbed over that.'

Mrs Lionel peered more closely at him. Although not much skin on his face showed, it had a deathly pallor. His bottom lip quivered, and altogether he seemed much less like a hulking biker and more like a little boy, albeit a hairy one, who had just received bad news. 'Sit,' she said, taking his arm and steering him to the couch. 'I'll get you tea.'

'Thank you,' he said, sinking into the cushions. 'I could do with a strong lapsang souchong.'

Mrs Lionel made the tea in one of her standard pots while she kept a close eye on the man. He sat very still on the couch, smooth dark hair visible over the top. Percy sat and watched him but his hackles weren't raised. Mrs Lionel decided that the man was, for the moment, harmless. She delivered his tea to the coffee table and sat in a chair to his side. 'The death of those men has upset you immensely.'

'Yes,' he said, grasping the teacup in both hands and sipping loudly.

'You knew them well?'

'Nah. I'm just an emotional type and I knew their story.' The man put his cup down. 'Thank you very much for this.'

'Harry!'

Mrs Lionel jumped. Another dark-haired man stood at the back door, clearly having jumped the railing as well.

Harry nodded towards him. 'That's Gordy. My brother.'

'Does he prefer lapsang souchong?'

'He's more of a bergamot man.'

'Earl Grey it is, then.'

Mrs Lionel indicated that Gordy join his brother, and then made another pot of tea. She watched the brothers as the kettle boiled, noting the similar smoothness of their hair as they put their heads together to talk. She carried a tray to the coffee table and set it down. 'Hello, Gordy. I am Mrs Lionel. Harry was about to tell me more about the twins' story.'

Gordy's eyebrows shot up. 'He was?'

'I was explaining to this lovely lady that we knew their story.'

Gordy scratched his beard. 'Rightio.'

'Tea?' asked Mrs Lionel, pouring the second man a cup. She handed it to him, noticing how his fingers shook as he took it. 'You both seem rather upset.'

'I'm upset, alright.' Gordy sipped his tea.

Harry raised the cup again and drained the lot in one gulp. Mrs Lionel leaned forward and poured him another. 'We're all upset,' he said. 'The sidecars were useful.'

'To carry the sacks of presents?'

'Yes.' Harry sighed. 'Ned made those sacks himself because he used them outside of Christmas time for his business.'

'What was his occupation?'

'He worked as a cleaner. The sacks were for his dirty laundry.'

'And what did his brother do?'

'Ted was an accountant.'

'A useful occupation.'

'You'd think so.' Harry lowered his head and stared at the floor. 'He had some big clients, he said. Science laboratories and such that he visited to do their books.'

After a long minute's silence, Mrs Lionel decided that Harry had said all he was going to say. She went to stand but his head came up and he looked at her. 'There's more, isn't there?' she said, settling back.

'Not really,' said Gordy.

Harry glanced at him. 'Well, there is.' He turned back to Mrs Lionel. 'Ted and Ned only met after their mother died. Lawyers connected them.'

'Was one of them adopted out?' Mrs Lionel asked. 'It happened sometimes with twins.'

'No. They were separated at birth. Ned went with the father, Ted with the mother. They'd been told their other parent had died and I guess they didn't have any reason to not believe it. And now their father has been dead for decades and their mother is dead, too.' Harry waved his hands around. 'Apparently, even though they had never seen each other before, they had matching beards right down to the same length.'

'How curious.'

'Yep, yep. The whole thing is curious.'

Gordy shifted in his seat. 'Anyway, that's their story. Not as weird as some.'

Mrs Lionel poured the last of the tea into Harry's cup. 'Their deaths have clearly upset you more than most.'

Harry rocked forward and took up the cup. 'Do you think so?'

Mrs Lionel strained to see out her glass doors to the balcony beyond. 'I don't see any other brothers leaping the railing and staggering inside a stranger's house. Except your own, of course.'

Harry blushed and his hand trembled slightly as he lowered his tea. 'I'm a sook,' he said.

'You are,' said Gordy. 'A big baby, like you've always been.'

Mrs Lionel put a hand out to stop Percy who had started a low growl.

'Well,' Harry said, swallowing, 'you see-'

'You see,' interrupted Gordy, 'we'd like to see them.'

'We would?'

Gordy nodded firmly but didn't look at his brother. 'We need to pay our last respects.'

'It's a crime scene, dear,' said Mrs Lionel. 'It wouldn't be wise. You might leave your DNA there.'

'We'll keep our DNA to ourselves.' Gordy stood. 'Won't we, Harry?'

'Yes,' said Harry, rising slowly. 'And we really should see them. Respectfully, like.'

Someone crashed through the door of The Green Mulbury, sending the frog into a croaky spin, and pounded across the wooden floor to the doorway leading into Mrs Lionel's living quarters. 'Mrs Lionel, darling!' called a high-pitched voice. 'Are you there?'

Mrs Lionel stood. 'Come in, Rakisha.'

'Oh, no, darling, I won't come in,' Rakisha said as she stepped into the lounge. 'I am on an errand. Rosemary was wondering where you were and I said I'd go and look and here you are, darling. With friends.' She smiled absently at Harry and Gordy.

'You can tell Rosemary that I'm okay, Rakisha.' Mrs Lionel picked up a tea tray. 'And could you ask her to escort our friends here to Mullings. They would like to-'

'Offer blessings to their departed comrades!' Rakisha pressed her palms together. 'Oh, darlings, you are lovely bikers.'

'We don't need a chaperone,' said Gordy.

'Well, I insist,' said Mrs Lionel. 'Rosemary knows the scene and therefore what shouldn't be disturbed.' She turned to Rakisha. 'Get Rosemary now.'

Rakisha blinked at Mrs Lionel's sharp tone, but turned on her heels, and exited in a flurry of cotton.

'That was unnecessary,' said Harry. 'We would be fine.'

'Totally unnecessary,' said Gordy, making for the door.

'Oh, it's no trouble.' Mrs Lionel moved so she was in between them. 'No problem at all.' She stumbled on the step to the shop, falling against Gordy who stopped to help her straighten. 'Thank you, dear. I'm not as good as I was on my old feet. Ah, look. Rosemary's here.'

Rosemary stood outside the door and the men had no choice but to allow her to join them. Mrs Lionel squeezed her arm before she left, getting a double squeeze back. As she went back into The Green Mulbury and silenced the frog, she turned to Percy. 'It's okay. We'll tell Rosemary all that they said. She'll keep an eye on them.'

The spectral dog stopped his low growl and wagged his tail. Mrs Lionel smiled at him as they walked back into the dining room. Percy was not the only one who felt confident that Rosemary Exeter would find out what Harry and Gordy were up to.

# SIX

The rain didn't let up as Rosemary led Gordy and Harry across the Square. The usually dry gravel had been shaped into channels and the rain turned them into small rivers. Rosemary jumped over the largest and weaved her way to Kelly's café where the inside lights shone like beacons against the dark grey clouds overhead. She pushed open the door and held it for the brothers.

Ned and Ted lay exactly as they'd been when Moose had dumped them out of their sacks, albeit with tablecloths draped half-heartedly over their torsos. With the advantage of a bit of distance, Rosemary saw how their limbs sprawled in almost identical ways but as if a mirror-image. Beside her, Harry wasn't so steady. His whole body shook until his brother gripped his shoulder and said in a fierce whisper, 'That's enough.'

'Gordy,' said Harry. 'Look at them.'

'I am looking.'

'But...' Harry seemed to remember Rosemary and glanced back at her, so she walked to stand against Kelly's counter.

Gordy crouched to look at the array of items Rosemary had pulled from their pockets. 'Who did this?' His sharp voice echoed around the room.

'I did,' said Rosemary.

'Shouldn't you have left it for the police?'

'Yes.'

He glared at her. 'And you're worried about *us* contaminating the scene.'

Rosemary shrugged. 'I was looking to see if they had any health concerns. Did they?'

'Why ask me?'

Harry crouched beside his brother. 'They must have. You don't die spontaneously unless you do.'

Rosemary watched him. 'Unless someone murdered them.'

Harry flinched. 'But there are no signs they did.'

Rosemary strained to check for bruises on the small sections of the men's skin that weren't covered in hair but failed. The ginger beards hid the men's necks entirely, with drooping moustaches covering their mouths. 'There might be once they're at the coroners.'

'Heart attack,' said Gordy.

'Both of them?' asked Rosemary.

'Genetically possible.'

'Statistically improbable.'

'Well.' Gordy leaned further over Ned, putting his hands either side of the dead man's head. 'It's not for us to say.' He pushed himself upright. 'Come on, Harry. Time to go.'

Harry let his brother pull him along.

'Finished what you came to do?' asked Rosemary.

The men stared at her.

She smiled at him. 'Paying your respects?'

Gordy gave a mirthless grin back and started for the door. 'Yes. We have.'

A flash of brilliant lightning made the cafe momentarily overbright but not before Rosemary saw Gordy slip something to Harry as they went out. She glanced back at the twins and paused.

'Coming?' said Gordy, his voice almost drowned out by a monstrous roll of thunder.

'In a moment.' Rosemary pointed back into the shop. 'Kelly wanted me to check her fridges. Sometimes they don't come back on when the power does.'

Gordy opened his mouth to say something, but she shut the door in his face, smiling reassuringly as she quietly flicked the lock. For a moment, it looked as if he might try to get back in, but the rain slanted down in earnest and he took off after Harry who was already halfway across the Square.

Rosemary retreated to the back of the shop where she had already heard the hum of happy fridges and waited until the men were back in The Preserved Mulbury. She ventured up to the twins again and crouched as Gordy had done. In this position, not only had he been directly over Ned's head, but his fingers had touched the items pulled from the men's pocket. Rosemary studied them. Timothy Armstrong's driver's licence was gone.

She sat back on her heels. Ned's head was slightly turned, with one of his moustaches sticking out in a way that didn't match the rest of his coiffured appearance. While Rosemary had no doubt that being dumped unceremoniously out of a sack would make anyone's moustache stick out, it seemed to be more than that. She leaned over him again and used a pencil from Kelly's counter to push the hair back lightly. It wasn't that the hair was sticking out, it was Ned's upper lip was protruding. She stuck the pencil in and carefully pushed his lip back, exposing what seemed to be a wad of something white wedged in his mouth. By twisting the pencil, the wad came out in a soggy lump and she placed it on a plate from one of the café tables. Paper?

Using the same technique, she twisted the pencil around Ted's slightly open mouth but it was empty. Scum stained his lips but at least his mouth was free.

Thunder crashed again, so close it shook the café. Rosemary stood and looked around at the grim scene. Bright presents scattered across the floor, the men's belongings patched in between, and the twins sprawled helplessly next to their sacks. Not the usual Christmas Eve scene.

A sharp rapping at the door made her turn, expecting to see Gordy and Harry demanding to enter. Instead, it was the white-bearded brothers, Bill and Rock. 'Let us in, will you?' asked Bill.

Rosemary hesitated. Although she hadn't meant it to become this way, the café was indeed a contaminated crime scene. Muddy footprints patterned the floor, and the air felt thick and fuggy. The scattering of presents and the carefully laid out contents of the twins' pockets didn't help.

The rapping became thudding. 'Come on. We're really wet.'

Rosemary studied the men through the door. They had similar features, but it was clear that Bill was the oldest. He pressed his face to the glass, making the deep lines in his face flatten. There was something manic about the look in his eyes and she didn't think it was all because water was running down his neck. She strode to the door and unlocked it. Bill almost fell in.

'Yeah, thanks,' he said. 'You could have done that ten minutes ago.'

'You weren't there ten minutes ago.'

'Lucky for us. We would have drowned.'

'It's not that bad,' said Rock, squeezing water out of his beard. 'We're in now.'

'You're in,' said Rosemary. 'What do you want?'

Rock glanced down at Ned and Ted. 'We just wanted to see them. You know? See for ourselves that they are...'

Rosemary put her hands on her hips. 'Dead?'

Rock shook his head slowly.

Bill nudged him aside and squatted at Ted's head. Rosemary moved back to give the men room, but also so she could watch what happened next. Bill reached a finger out and touched Ted's cheek, withdrawing it almost immediately. 'Softer than I thought,' he said quietly.

'Don't,' said Rock. 'That's disrespectful.'

Bill looked up at his brother, turning his face away from Rosemary so she didn't see the expression on his face. Rock's reaction was clear. He stepped back and rubbed his face.

Bill twisted to see Rosemary. 'This one's the accountant.'

'Apparently.'

He pointed to Ned. 'And that one's the thief.'

Rosemary raised an eyebrow. 'He was a cleaner, so I've been told.'

'Yeah.' Bill huffed. 'A cleaner, all right. Cleaned everything right away, didn't he?'

Rock came forward and bent over to put a heavy hand on his brother's back. 'Bill, the man is dead.'

Bill pushed himself quickly to standing. 'Doesn't make what he did any better because he's dead.'

Rock shook his head. 'It's all over now. Let it go.'

'No.' Bill stepped over Ted's arm to get to Ned. 'I can't!'

'Let what go?' asked Rosemary as Bill's shout died down. 'What did Ned do?'

'He didn't do anything to us,' said Rock. 'But we found out what he did to others.'

'Which was?'

Rock shrugged. 'He took things from people's houses. The houses he was there to clean.'

'What sorts of things?'

'Antiques. Jewellery. Money.'

'He was reported to the police?'

Rock shook his head. 'No. We had our own way of dealing with him.' He jabbed fingers at the parcels on the floor. 'We made him buy the Christmas presents.'

'All of them?'

'Most. Some were donated.'

'And that resolved the matter?'

'Yes,' said Rock.

'No,' said Bill. He twisted the end of his beard around one finger.

Rock chewed his lip for a moment then turned to Rosemary. 'My brother,' he said. 'He's a good man usually. He doesn't like when evil things happen to people who don't deserve it.'

Rosemary nodded. 'Like robbing vulnerable people's houses.'

'Yes,' said Rock. 'Exactly.' He clapped Bill's back. 'We had a nickname for him when we were kids. Hoody.'

'As in the clothing?'

'As in Robin Hood.'

'Taking from the rich and giving to the poor?'

Rock shrugged. 'He didn't take anything, did you, Bill? It was all talk. He was always saying how we need to look out for each other and take special care of those who couldn't look after themselves. He's a bit of a softy, is Bill.'

*Soft he may be,* thought Rosemary as she studied the look of revulsion on Bill's face as he stared at Ned, *but there's also something very tough inside him.* 'How did you find out?'

Rock frowned. 'Find out what?'

'That Ned was taking things from people's homes. You said you didn't know him very well.'

'Oh.' Rock crossed his arms. 'We found out when we went to their house.'

'Why did that matter?'

Bill shook his head suddenly 'Because it was all there! All the stuff he'd stolen. Lined up on the floor, on tables, against the wall. Boxes of watches, rows of clocks, those pottery ladies.' He gestured at the dead man. 'I knew as soon as I walked in that it wasn't right. I said so, didn't I, Rock?'

'You did. You said the same to Ted.'

'But not Ned?' The rain had started again and Rosemary had to raise her voice. 'You didn't say anything to Ned?'

'He wasn't there. We'd come to see Ted.'

'They lived together?'

Rock nodded. 'They'd been living in the family home since their mum died. Ted had his accountancy business running from the front room.'

'That's why you were there?'

Thunder rolled overhead, stopping Rosemary from hearing Bill's next words. Rock rubbed his face again and took a little step back to gaze out of the window. 'This rain,' Rock said. 'It's getting on my nerves.'

*Something is getting on your nerves,* Rosemary thought.

'Ted was your accountant as well?' she asked.

'Yeah, he was an accountant for both of us.'

'Good, was he?'

Bill glanced at Rock and frowned. 'Very good.'

'You don't seem very happy about that.'

Rock ran a hand over his chin and through his beard, leaving a few long hairs to drift to the floor. 'Well, when we saw what Ned had been up to...'

'...and that it was obvious Ted knew...'

'...we thought that Ted might have been more *accommodating* with our situation, seeing as he clearly relished his brother's little venture.'

'What was your situation?'

Rock's face hardened. 'Nosey, aren't ya?'

Rosemary shrugged. 'Just trying to make sense of all that's happened.'

'Yeah, right.' Rock shook his head. 'Don't think we had anything to do with that.' He pointed to the twins. 'We wanted Ted to help us through tough times.'

'You wanted him to cook the books for you?'

'That's blunt,' said Bill.

'It's correct, isn't it?'

Rock and Bill looked at each other. Bill scrubbed at his head. 'Well, he wouldn't. He's a hypocrite.'

'*Was* a hypocrite,' said Rosemary.

'Was.' Bill nodded. 'Yep. And now we have no one to...' he eyeballed Rosemary '...adjust our bookkeeping.'

'Because you feel you belong to that section of people you always looked out for.'

Bill frowned. 'The government gets too much money and leaves nothing for us.' He crossed his arms. 'So, we're entitled to keep it.'

'Right.'

'So, you agree?' Rock took an eager step forward. 'Do you know anyone who would, you know, help us out?'

After a minute of complete silence, in which Rosemary listed in her head the many things that taxes pay for in the public arena, the white-bearded bikers got the message and backed slowly out of the café.

Rosemary waited until they had crossed the Square before she turned back to the wad of paper on the plate. It was drying slowly but some black letters already stood out. '...ax,' she read, poking the wad carefully until another letter was revealed. 'Tax.'

Someone had stoppered Ted's mouth with a tax return.

# SEVEN

Rosemary ran back through the teeming rain to The Preserved Mulbury. She jumped the gutter, slipped on its concrete edge, and landed squarely in Jasper's arms.

'Oops,' he said, face dissolving into crimson.

She straightened and extracted herself. 'Sorry. I misjudged that one.'

'That's okay,' said Jasper, his hands out as if she was going to slip again. 'I'm here.'

'Yes.' She eyeballed him. 'What else is up? You look guilty.'

'Oh.' Jasper wiped the hair out of his eyes and hooked it behind his ears. 'Do I? Not guilty, more...'

'Compromised? What did you do?'

'I didn't do anything. I was just standing there. They talked in front of me.'

'Who did?'

'Those men.' Jasper indicated the shop behind him. 'The white-haired ones.'

'Bill and Rock. What did they say?'

Jasper took Rosemary's elbow and led her away to his shop front. 'Best to keep away when I tell you.'

'Jasper, we're the only ones under the veranda.'

'What about them?'

Rosemary looked where he was pointing. The rows of motorbikes took up most of the path, their tanks dark in the dim light. 'They're inanimate objects.'

'Even so.' He pushed open the door of The Read Mulbury and steered her inside.

The shop was cool despite the clammy weather. Rosemary followed Jasper as he wove his way around bookshelves and display tables until they reached his lounge room. Snowy wagged his tail from his upside spot on the couch. She gave his belly a rub and he returned a doggy smile before falling back asleep.

'Tea?' asked Jasper from the kitchen.

'Jasper, you were going to tell me something.'

'I will. I thought you might like tea, though. You always like tea.'

She sighed quietly at the disappointment in his voice. 'Yes, tea would be lovely. A Darjeeling if you have it. And do you have any of Franco's Florentines?'

'One left. You're lucky.'

Rosemary wandered into the little kitchen and sat at Jasper's wooden table. He set a scarlet teapot down and slid the biscuit onto a plate before putting it in front of her. She drummed her fingers on her leg until he finally sat down himself.

'Right,' she said, helping herself to the tea. 'Tell me.'

'They came back from Mullings and stood outside for a while.' Jasper nodded as she offered to pour him a cup. 'I went out to give them sandwiches. They didn't want any. In fact, they waved me away.' He imitated an impatient hand gesture.

'Rude.'

'I thought so. Anyway, I had to clean up and that's when I heard them talking.'

'Clean up what?'

'I dropped the sandwiches.'

Rosemary studied Jasper's innocent face as he sipped tea. He had the benefit of deep brown eyes framed by thick eyelashes, but she wasn't fooled. 'You dropped those sandwiches deliberately.'

He shrugged. 'They fell from the plate. Bad luck, really.'

'I see.'

'Anyway, it took me a while to pick them up. Your curried pickles make quite a mess when they hit the ground.'

'I see.'

'The tall one said, "It was there, on the table. I saw it." The shorter one said, "How did it get there?" The other one said, "I have no idea."'

Rosemary sipped her tea, imagining the café scene in front of her. 'There was a wad of paper I pulled out of Ned's mouth. I left it on a plate.'

'What sort of paper?'

'A tax return. What else did they say?'

'"She didn't twig."'

'Who didn't twig?'

'Rosemary, you were the only *she* there, weren't you? I assume they meant you.'

'They'd be right. I didn't twig it was a tax return until after they left.'

Jasper reached over and broke the Florentine in two,

taking the smaller half. 'You twigged about something, though.'

'There was no love between those pairs of brothers. That was obvious.' She took the other half of the biscuit. 'Bill and Rock think Ned was a disreputable character, but Ted wasn't disreputable enough. Ned stole things from the houses they cleaned. They wanted Ted to put in a false tax form.'

'Oh, okay then. Lots of dodginess there. Were Bill and Rock cheesed off enough to put Ned and Ted out of action permanently?'

Rosemary nibbled the biscuit. 'Someone in that group was or we wouldn't have two dead bodies in Kelly's café.'

'Someone or a couple. They come in twos, those brothers.'

'Yes.'

They sat for a quiet moment, the only noises the smattering of rain on the kitchen window and contended Snowy snores.

Jasper crunched the last of his Florentine, breaking their silence. 'What's next?'

As if to answer, rain belted down again, followed by thunder. It gave Rosemary another moment to think. 'The police won't be here for ages,' she shouted over the noise. 'In the meantime, we have a bunch of people here, some of whom may be murderers.'

Jasper's face paled. 'What are you going to do, Rosemary?'

'I'm going to do more thinking. Starting with the book.'

'Which book?'

'The one we first took. The Shakespeare. Have you got it here?'

'Hang on.' He stood up from the table and disappeared

into his bedroom, coming back with the tatty book that looked so much like another tatty book recently found. Rosemary took it from him and opened it to the dedication. 'To my darling T,' she read, then tapped it. 'That T is for Tommy.'

'I thought it was for Ted?'

She shook her head. 'I found another one in the sidecar. These were Tommy's books, not Ted's.'

'Tommy's?'

'Tommy and Moose swapped the computers for books.'

'They were stealing them?'

'Yes.'

Jasper hooked his hair behind one ear and stared down at the table. 'You know...'

Rosemary waited but he was quiet. She rapped her knuckles against the teapot. 'What, Jasper? Speak up.'

'Sorry. Miles away...'

Rosemary tugged his sleeve. 'What is it, Jasper? Is there something about that book?'

He slowly turned to her. 'You haven't read it?'

'No. It wasn't on my high school reading list all those decades ago. You'll have to tell me what you're thinking.'

Jasper smiled. 'Not so many decades ago.'

'It is, Jasper. Face it. It's been decades for both of us. Now. The book?'

He nodded. 'Shakespeare featured the dynamics of siblings a lot in his plays. Sometimes they get on, sometimes they don't. In fact, there was a lot of sibling rivalry in his plays. King Lear. As you Like It. The Tempest. A few examples.'

'What are you saying, Jasper?'

'Well, I was just thinking that not all brothers like each other.'

'I still don't get what you're saying.'

'I wasn't saying anything, really. Just that sometimes siblings don't get on with each other.'

'Like you don't get on with Helena, your sister.'

'Half-sister. And it's not that we don't get on...'

'It's just that she bosses you around.' Rosemary leaned back. 'I get it. Are you suggesting, though, that one of our bearded brother pairs don't get on as well as we think?'

Jasper shrugged. 'No idea. It was only a passing comment.' He lifted the tea pot. 'More tea?'

'No. Thanks.' She stood to go. 'I need to go.'

Jasper glanced around at his bottle-green kitchen as if he'd find something to keep her there.

'I'm going, Jasper,' she said. 'You need to take Snowy out.' She gestured at the doorway of the kitchen where the old dog stood slowly wagging his tail, his head on one side, gazing up at his master.

She felt, rather than saw, Jasper's lingering gaze as she exited through the bookshop. Sibling rivalry, eh? It was something else to go on.

# EIGHT

Rosemary went back to The Preserved Mulbury but didn't go inside. The sound of the rain on veranda roof created a lovely lot of white noise, allowing her to do some thinking standing where she was without needing to find a quiet place.

A repeated jangle from the door behind her finally forced her to look around. Mrs Lionel came out of the shop, stepping carefully onto the asphalt. Rosemary nodded a greeting to her friend, and together they watched the water cascading from the veranda gutter. 'Haven't seen it like this ever,' said Mrs Lionel. 'What do you think?'

'I think one of them was poisoned and the other asphyxiated.'

'I imagine we're no longer talking about the weather.'

'No.' Rosemary turned to her friend. 'Sorry, thinking about other things, such as what killed the two men. Hypothetically.'

'Well, dear,' said Mrs Lionel. 'Your hypotheses are usually close to truth. What makes you say this?'

'Ted has dried white scum on his lips.'

'As if he'd been frothing.'

'Yes. That's a sign of poisoning.'

'Among other things.'

'Tell me about those other things.'

Mrs Lionel frowned. 'Let me think back to my nurse training. Frothing or foaming at the mouth is a very uncommon symptom. As we don't have rabies in this country, it usually meant someone was having a seizure or it was a drug overdose.'

'Poisoning?'

'Poisoning would be considered a drug overdose. However, Ted may also have had a fit of some kind. They said he looked under the weather.' Mrs Lionel shook her head. 'Mind you, that could mean anything. Ned was asphyxiated?'

'He had a wad of paper in his mouth.'

'That's odd.'

'That's suspicious.'

'It is indeed. But a wad of paper alone wouldn't be enough to asphyxiate a full-grown man.'

Rosemary shifted back as the gutter let loose a torrent of water and leaves, taking Mrs Lionel with her to save her from being splashed. 'You know chemicals.'

'I'm not a chemist.'

'But you've worked on a farm and you mix things up in your shop all the time.'

'Natural ingredients, dear.'

'Some of which could be poisonous if used incorrectly.'

'Yes, that's true of most things.'

'So, what sort of poisons might Ted have come into contact with?'

'I have no idea. What did he do for a living?'

'He was an accountant.' Rosemary put a finger on her friend's arm. 'But Ned was a cleaner.'

Mrs Lionel nodded. 'Cleaners use chemicals. To kill someone would mean that they ingested a lot. It's unlikely that someone would willingly swallow chemicals.'

'Unlikely. Unless they didn't know they were doing it.'

'True. If someone had mixed the poison in a drink, for example, or had drugged the person in the first place. I have seen nasty cases like that in the news.' Mrs Lionel shrugged. 'But who would have done that to our two dead gentlemen? And why?'

'I'm not sure. Yet.'

'A penny for your thoughts, dear.'

'They may not be worth that much.'

'Try me.'

Rosemary crossed her arms and gazed out into the rain. 'The presents in the sacks were meant to be technological gadgets, computers and tablets. And yet they are books.'

'Books? Any particular ones?'

'Old ones. Second hand ones. Tommy's ones.'

'Tommy's?'

'Yes. Ones that we've found had his name in them.' Rosemary rubbed her arms as a sharp gust of wind blew rain towards her. 'Moose and Tommy were in charge of wrapping those particular presents.'

'Ah.' Mrs Lionel shook her head. 'Interesting.'

'Yes, but it's not the only thing. The driver's licence of Timothy Armstrong is missing.'

'Missing?'

'I suspect Gordy took it when he and Harry came to see the bodies.'

'Why on earth would he do that?'

'I'm not sure. It's a good question.'

Mrs Lionel frowned. 'So, we have some unusual activity going on with some of the bearded brothers.'

'Yes.' Rosemary turned at the noise of a jangling door and bent close to Mrs Lionel's ear. 'And here come the last two.'

Bill and Rock stepped out of The Preserved Mulbury. Bill glanced towards the Square before nodding at the women. 'Ladies.' He tipped his head.

'Gentlemen,' said Rosemary.

Bill smiled briefly at Rosemary, and walked away to the end of the veranda, Rock following. They stood with their heads together talking, Rosemary watching intently. 'The wad of paper was a tax form.'

'Is that significant?'

'Only if the owner didn't like what was on it.'

Mrs Lionel sighed. 'I feel like I'm only getting half the picture, Rosemary Exeter. How about we go into my shop for a while and you can tell me everything you're thinking.'

Rosemary followed Mrs Lionel into The Green Mulbury, stretching around the older woman to hold the door as her went inside. The electronic frog croaked incessantly until the door swung shut behind her. She watched as Mrs Lionel bent over something on the floor, talking quietly as if to a loved one.

'How is Percy?' asked Rosemary stepping forward as her friend straightened.

'He's grand.' Mrs Lionel smiled at the floor. 'He's wagging his tail at you.'

Rosemary fixed her eyes on the empty floor. 'Hello, Percy.'

Mrs Lionel tugged her dress straight. 'You don't have to humour me, dear. I know you can't see him.'

'I was being nice.'

'Yes, well, stop it. It doesn't suit you.' Mrs Lionel sent a cheeky grin to Rosemary before turning to go into her living area. 'Now, tell me what all those strange thoughts are in your head.'

Rosemary went to Mrs Lionel's dining table and pulled out a straight-backed chair to sit on as the kettle clunked onto its hob. 'Not so strange. Only a little disordered at the moment. I suspect, though, we could have several suspects among the brothers.'

'Suspected suspects?' Mrs Lionel chuckled then sobered. 'Oh, I shouldn't laugh. That's terrible of me. Two men are dead, we're probably harbouring murderers, and with the way this rain is going, we're probably not going to see any police until next year.'

The thought of being stuck with the Bearded Biker Brothers in her house for more than a day made Rosemary frown. *Sunny would go spare,* she thought. 'We just have to work out which of the brothers we won't be able to trust.'

Mrs Lionel filled a silver teapot. 'You implied that none of them could be trusted.'

'Yes. We need to discover the least trustworthy.' Rosemary stood to take the tea tray from her friend. 'I've only just had tea with Jasper.'

'You can't have too much tea,' said Mrs Lionel. 'Especially when you need to think hard.'

Rosemary couldn't argue with that logic. She swirled the pot a few times before pouring two cups.

'Right, dear, now tell me what you're really thinking.'

Rosemary raised her cup but didn't get a chance to sip before someone knocked heavily on the door to The Green

Mulbury. She glanced at a puzzled Mrs Lionel and put her cup down. 'I'll get it.'

The lights were off in the shop and the day remained gloomy, so it was difficult to see who exactly was at the door, although the heavy outline of two large men meant it could only be a pair of brothers. As she got closer, she saw the dark heads of Harry and Gordy. She opened the door, the frog accompanying her with its croaky tune, and the men stepped back.

'Oh,' said Gordy. 'You aren't the old lady.'

Rosemary bristled. 'There is no old lady here.'

'Sorry, sorry.' Gordy scratched his cheek. 'I meant the woman who lives here.'

'Mrs Lionel.'

'Mrs Lionel, yes.'

'What do you want with her?'

Gordy glared at his brother. 'Harry left something here when he...visited.'

'What did he leave?'

'It's hard to describe.' Gordy peered around Rosemary. 'I thought we could have a quick look inside.'

Rosemary looked at Harry, who had the grace to turn away from her inquiring stare. 'I'll check. Just a moment.' She shut the door on the men and went back to Mrs Lionel.

'Who is it, dear?'

'The brothers who visited you before. They say they've left something behind.'

'Really?' Mrs Lionel scraped her chair back. 'I didn't see anything.'

'Stay there. I'll have a look.'

Mrs Lionel nodded, picking the pot up to pour more tea. 'See what you can find.'

Rosemary went to where the men had sat. Apart from

the scatter of cushions disturbed from having two large men sit on them, the couch looked the same as always. She knelt and ran her hand along the edge of the couch, feeling down its side for any hint of a lost thing. Nothing. She bent lower and felt underneath the couch.

The first thing she pulled out was a man's hanky. She dropped it in disgust and stuck her arm back under. She almost didn't notice the second thing as her hand slid across the top, but its coolness made her pause. She curled her fingers over the top and pulled something out. 'Ah,' she said.

'What is it?' asked Mrs Lionel from her place at the table.

'A business card wallet.' She opened it. 'With business cards in it.'

'For what business?'

'*Identicals*.'

'What sort of business is that?'

Rosemary turned a card over. 'I don't know. Besides a phone number and a website, that's the only thing it says.'

'Odd. Do you think that's what they're looking for?'

'There's a hanky here.' Rosemary held it up by one corner. 'I'm supposing it isn't yours.'

Mrs Lionel shook her head. 'Definitely not. Are you going to let them in?'

Rosemary dropped the hanky onto the back of the couch and slipped the business card into her pocket before going back to the door and ushering the men in. 'Mrs Lionel didn't find anything of yours except a handkerchief. You're welcome to have a look yourself.'

Gordy pushed Harry in the back and he strode into Mrs Lionel's living area. Rosemary hung back, hearing the greetings of the men and the sound of cushions being patted in a similar way to how she had done it moments before. She went to stand behind Mrs Lionel's shop counter and pulled the business card from her pocket, quickly dialling the number on it. A pause, and then another phone rang coming from Mrs Lionel's lounge room.

'Feel free to answer that, dear,' said Mrs Lionel from her kitchen.

A split second later, a voice boomed through Rosemary's phone speaker while at the same time being echoed in the room behind her. 'Hello, Harrison from *Identicals* here.'

Rosemary ended the call.

'Hello?' said Harry. 'They've gone.'

'Wrong number, dear?' Mrs Lionel rattled cups onto the kitchen bench.

Harry didn't answer, or not that Rosemary heard. She was on Mrs Lionel's shop computer swiftly looking up the Identicals website. There was only time to read the first line before Gordy was back in the shop, looking at her suspiciously. She changed the screen. 'Find what you were looking for?' she asked.

'No.' He stepped forward, glancing at the computer.

'What have you lost? We could keep an eye out for it.' She indicated the doorway into the house. 'Although I'm assuming the hanky is yours.'

'Yeah, he got that. Where was it?'

'On the floor.'

'Nothing else with it?'

'Like what?'

Gordy wriggled his shoulders. 'Pocket contents. You know.'

'What, car keys? Wallet? Old receipts?'

'Yeah. Stuff like you'd find in pockets. Anyway.' Gordy

whistled once, and Harry appeared in the doorway. 'We're going to check the bikes.'

Rosemary waited until they'd gone out the croaking door. She unplugged the laptop from the counter and took it to Mrs Lionel who sat at the table once more. 'Look,' Rosemary said, placing the computer in front of her friend.

'"Identicals",' read Mrs Lionel. '"The website for novelty fake IDs. Overnight cards for you."' She looked at Rosemary. 'They were looking for a lost business card about making fake identification?'

'*Their* fake identification business. It was me ringing Harry using the number on the card.'

'Well,' said Mrs Lionel, tapping the computer screen. 'It says they produce novelty cards without any government symbols or anything. I don't think those sorts of things are illegal unless they're used illegally by the person receiving them.'

'No, you're right there. But you remember Timothy Armstrong?'

'The driver's licence fellow?'

'That's the one. And now it's missing. Strange?'

'Strange.' Mrs Lionel yawned. 'Sorry, dear, but I am very tired today. It's been long and hot.'

'Why don't you rest for a while?'

'And leave you alone to sort this out?' Mrs Lionel smiled but a second yawn twisted it. 'Sorry, dear.'

'Stop apologising and rest up.'

'Alright.' Mrs Lionel stood and started making her way to her bedroom, patting her leg so that the ghostly Percy went with her.

Rosemary waited until she heard the creak of the bed, and let herself out quietly, slipping back into The Preserved Mulbury. The rain had eased again, and the six burly bikers sat outside on her porch surrounded by mugs and plates of biscuits. Rosemary frowned. She thought they'd finished all the biscuits in the house. The fragrance of ginger and cinnamon wafting from her kitchen, though, proved that supplies had been renewed.

Jules stood at the sink and turned at Rosemary's entrance. She had her blonde hair pulled back in a clasp, and the ivory-coloured linen dress she wore was covered with one of Rosemary's large floral aprons. 'Rosemary, I'm so sorry.'

'Whatever for?'

Jules indicated a row of cake racks on which multitudes of biscuits lay cooling. 'I thought I'd whip up a few sweets for the men as they seem to be eating you out of house and home.'

'You found everything you needed in the pantry?'

Jules used an elegant finger to push a strand of hair from her eyes. 'Yes. And, I know, I could have done this at home but I'm so worried...' She ducked her head to the dishes.

'There's no word about Roman.'

'No.'

'And you didn't want to be at home. Alone.'

Jules scrubbed at a cooking tray. 'There's nothing else to be done at present. The police are busy with other more dramatic events. Gerry and Patti are driving around as much as they can with so much water on the roads. I'm sure Roman has his phone on silent and hasn't checked it.' She smiled, the corners of her mouth wobbling. 'It will work out.'

Rosemary pulled another apron from the hook behind the pantry door and picked up a tea towel without commenting. Roman had been gone most of the day, which was a worry that hadn't been lost on Jules.

'I just wish...' Jules swirled the soapy water in front of her. 'I just wish he'd shared whatever's going on with him. With me. He could have shared it with me.'

'I know he could. He knows he could, too. Maybe he's not ready, though.'

Jules nodded. 'I hear you, Rosemary. I must wait.'

Rosemary put her hand briefly on Jules's arm. 'I'm sure he'll be okay.'

Jules sniffed and swallowed before glancing briefly at Rosemary. 'Was this like when...'

'When Alasdair went missing?' Rosemary shook her head. 'Alasdair is not a bit like Roman. He was, and remains, unpredictable. I should have guessed he could disappear if he wanted to without actually being in danger to himself or others. Just as I should have guessed that eventually he would turn up again.' She shrugged. 'Every Christmas, he sends me a letter, which I never read.'

'Never?'

'Not to date. I find them on my doorstep and put them away in a drawer.'

'Understandable.' Jules put a cooking tray on the draining rack. 'I know you always shrug it off, Rosemary,' she said softly. 'But it must have hurt when he went away like that, never intending to come back.'

Rosemary hesitated then pulled the tray roughly from the rack to dry. 'It was like being cut to the bone with a vicious knife.' She balanced the tray against the wall near her hotplates for it to air dry. 'But, with time, you can recover.'

'Apparently.' Jules gave her a small smile.

'Apparently.' Rosemary nodded. 'Doesn't mean it doesn't scar.' She went to shrug again and stopped herself. 'Anyway, the same thing will not happen to you. Roman is

Roman. Dependable. Apart from burning a few things, what was he acting like before today? Was he talking about anything unusual? Did he have something on his mind?'

Jules stopped washing up and stood for a moment with both hands in the water. 'It has been a hard year for him with his mother dying. She was in her nineties, but that doesn't make it any easier, does it?'

'It's still very sad.'

Jules pulled the plug, swirling the dirty water on its way down the sink. 'We had gone back to see her before she died, and then Roman travelled for the funeral. That was a few months ago now. He was quieter when he got back, but it didn't stop him cooking.'

'If Roman stopped cooking, the world is ending.'

Jules smiled more broadly. 'Indeed. I didn't worry too much about him, but as it got closer to Christmas, he became very sorrowful.' She put both hands on the sink edge. 'He kept telling me this story...'

'What story, Jules?'

'About Christmas in the vineyard when his grandparents were alive.' She looked up. 'They were vintners.'

'Right.'

'His grandmother made a vegetable dish only at Christmas time. When she died, his mother made it. It became their special family Christmas dish.'

'Which I'm sure Roman made for your family once he came here.'

'Well, that's it. He never did.' Jules straightened, smoothing her apron and patting her hair in place. 'He said that he wanted to start a new family tradition and so we always have a baked cheese Roman calls Capriccio Camembert. Felicity makes it for the kids if they don't spend Christmas with us.'

'So, you've never tasted this special vegetable dish?'

Jules shook her head. 'I only heard the story of Nonna's Christmas bake. When I asked him once why he couldn't make it at least once so that we knew what it tasted like, he said he couldn't get the ingredients.'

'Which ingredients?'

'Cardoons.'

'Never heard of them.'

'Not something we commonly have in this country.' Jules untied her apron and pulled it from her head. 'All this talk of Roman and I realise I haven't been home for a while. Maybe he's returned and I'm worrying for nothing?'

'Go and check. Come back here if you need to.'

Jules leaned over to plant a kiss on Rosemary's cheek. 'Thank you. Everyone is being so lovely.'

Rosemary managed not to pull back from her friend's display of emotion and felt the kiss as a prickly but well intended gesture. Jules noticed her discomfort and smiled wanly.

'Sorry, Rosemary. I forget that you aren't a particularly huggy person.'

'No, Jules, I'm sorry. But it is just the way I am.'

Jules put a light hand on Rosemary's arm. 'And how you are is how we like you.' She dropped her hand. 'I'll see you soon.'

Rosemary watched as Jules walked through the lounge area and into the shop, hearing the jangle of the door and the soft thud as it closed. Jules always walked with grace, head high and shoulders back, but it was a dejected version of that leaving The Preserved Mulbury.

'Excuse me.'

Rosemary shook her head clear of Jules's distress and turned to the voice. It was the mutton-chopped biker,

Moose. He held an empty plate out and she took it automatically.

'Sorry, I just didn't know where you wanted the dirty dishes,' he said.

'On the bench is fine,' said Rosemary. 'I'll show you how to operate the dishwasher when everyone is done.'

Moose laughed but stopped quickly when he saw Rosemary's raised eyebrow. 'Oh, yeah, sure. I don't have one at home but I'm sure I'll catch on.'

'Yes, you will.' Rosemary bent to put the plate in the machine. When she straightened, he was still staring at her. 'Can I help you with anything else?'

'Have you heard if the police are on their way?'

Rosemary glanced out the back door to the pelting rain ricocheting off the outside decking. 'No. I imagine they're still flooded in.'

'We may have to stay the night.'

'Yes.'

Moose put his hands in his jean's pockets. 'We won't all fit in here.'

'You could. We'll gather camping mattresses and you can sleep in the lounge or the spare bedroom.'

'Are you sure that's okay?'

She tilted her head. 'Do you have an alternative?'

'Not really. I was thinking of a bed and breakfast or a motel or something...' Moose shrugged.

'On Christmas Eve in this weather?'

The barely bare skin in front of his mutton chops reddened. 'It was just a thought.'

'You're welcome to try for better accommodation, but you are also welcome to stay here.' *Where I can keep an eye on you,* thought Rosemary. 'You will have to hang around until the police arrive anyway.'

'Yeah, yup, I get that.' Moose scratched his chops. 'And the local police...are they good?'

'Do you mean, will they solve the crime?'

'Yeah, I guess that's what I meant.'

Rosemary held Moose's gaze until he dropped his. 'I have no doubt about that at all.'

# NINE

Evening descended in a roar of pelting rain and menacing thunder. The lights flickered but stayed on, and Rosemary was able to continue concocting supper from the meagre stores she had left after hosting six burly men for a day. The supply of eggs and cream she'd purchased from Justin only the day before was almost gone, but she scrambled them together with some of his prime bacon to produce an almost Roman-esque fettucine carbonara.

Mrs Lionel nodded at the heaped plate of pasta as Rosemary carried it to the table. 'That reminds me. No news of Roman?'

'No.'

'Gerry and Patti are back, looking very bedraggled. No luck there.'

'Where did they search?'

'As far as they could while avoiding the water over the road.' Mrs Lionel shrugged and set the table with bowls for the bikers. 'Which wouldn't have been far.'

'They took their time.'

'Patti was also searching for abandoned garments, as she is wont to do. Apparently, she found two pairs of shorts and a hat swept into the gutter.'

'No doubt she'll turn those into something extraordinary for her shop.' Rosemary clapped her hands once. 'Supper, everyone.'

The six men stormed for the table as if it had been one week and not one hour since they'd eaten anything. Sunny poked her nose out of Rosemary's bedroom at the noise, and swiftly turned her back to the room, tail aloft. *Not going out there until these invaders are gone,* the tail clearly said.

'Does Jules know they're back?' Rosemary asked Mrs Lionel as they settled into their chairs.

'Yes. Poor dear. She's quite frantic but there's nothing anyone can do for now.' Mrs Lionel looked around the table. 'Is Jasper joining us?'

'No. He has a Christmas conference call with his sisters tonight. *Half*-sisters.'

'His only family.' Mrs Lionel picked up her fork. 'Christmas either brings people together or forces them apart. I'm glad, for Jasper, it's the former.'

Rosemary nodded as she ladled pasta into Mrs Lionel's bowl before filling her own. There was just enough to go around, and she was glad Mrs Lionel had found some focaccia to go with it. Moose raised his glass to her. 'Excellent mosh.'

The other bikers did the same, mumbling their gratitude through mouthfuls of food. Rosemary waited until they'd nearly finished then laid down her fork. 'So,' she said, sitting back. 'How did you all meet and become the Bearded Biker Brothers?'

Tommy gulped down a glass of water before wiping the

back of his hand with his mouth. 'Coincidence, really. And a love of bikes, of course.'

'What do you mean by coincidence?'

Tommy glanced at his brother. 'We met Bill and Rock at the local pub's dart competition. They had paired games that we played after work.'

'What is your work?'

'We fix electronics.' Tommy shrugged. 'Mainly household gadgets. Vacuum cleaners, beaters, stuff like that.'

'That's interesting, dear,' said Mrs Lionel. 'It's nice to know that if my old mixer breaks down, I could get it fixed.'

'Or buy a second hand one from us.' Moose grunted as his brother elbowed him.

'You sell electronics as well?' asked Rosemary.

'Only when we can get them,' said Moose, earning another nudge.

Rosemary looked at Tommy. 'Oh,' he said, smiling at Mrs Lionel without any mirth. 'We don't sell much. Wouldn't want to get your hopes up if your mixer does break down.'

'Well, there's no sign of it doing that for now.' Mrs Lionel turned to Bill and Rock. 'Do you have electronics in common as well as darts?'

'Electronics, us? No, no.' Rock shook his head. 'We're property investors.'

'You buy and sell real estate?'

'Yeah, we do.'

'That must take a lot of skill.'

'Or luck, eh?' said Harry. 'Haven't seen you making much of a living out of it yet.'

'We're waiting for the right moment,' said Rock, spinning his fork in his fingers.

'And what about you, dears?' said Mrs Lionel to Harry and Gordy. 'Are you electronics experts or investors?'

'Not us,' said Gordy.

'Oh, so you play darts then?'

'We were the bartenders at the pub,' said Harry. 'We had to look out for these lads when they got loutish.'

'Did that happen often?'

'Only every other night.'

Moose grinned. 'We didn't turn up every night.'

'We know.' Harry raised his glass to Moose. 'Every second night was quiet.'

'You're talking in the past tense,' said Rosemary. 'Don't you tend the bar anymore?'

Harry took a hasty drink. Gordy answered Rosemary. 'We've moved into our own business.'

'Ah.' Rosemary took a delicate sip of her water. *The fake ID industry must be quite lucrative,* she thought. She tipped her head at the other bikers. 'Do you still play darts?'

'No. The competition closed.' Rock scratched his chin. 'We really only meet now at this time of the year.'

'For the Cracker Christmas Kid's Charity. It's a big charity and they were looking for delivery people all over the state.'

'Yeah. We all joined it back in our darts playing days.'

'And Ned and Ted?'

'They came along much later with their sidecars.' Rock looked at Bill. 'I guess we won't have them next year.'

'Nuh, probably not. We'll have to make do with our panniers.'

Rosemary glanced at Mrs Lionel, who raised her eyebrows at Bill's casual tone. The sadness and shock of the twins' deaths seemed to have worn off completely. Tommy and Moose were wrestling over the last piece of bread, punching each other jokingly on the arm. Bill and Rock started a conversation about pannier volumes. Harry and Gordy finished their suppers, scooping pasta into their mouths as if they had shovels.

Rosemary folded her napkin in half and placed it on the table. 'I imagine Ned or Ted knew what each of you were up to.'

The men froze, Tommy and Moose with half the bread each in their hands, Bill and Rock mid-sentence, and Harry and Gordy with forks in their hands. 'Sorry?' said Bill into the stunned silence.

'Ned or Ted, or maybe Ned *and* Ted. Both could have been on to you all.' Rosemary felt Mrs Lionel's hand on her arm but ploughed on. She pointed to Tommy and Moose. 'They hid in the sacks for the sidecars and maybe they discovered you two had substituted books for computers.' Over the men's protests, she changed her pointer to Bill and Rock. 'You two had been fiddling with your investments, a fact discovered by Ted when he looked at your books as your accountant.' She moved her finger to Harry and Gordy. 'And Ned knew that some of your IDs were more than novelty items.' She sat back, folding her arms. 'Any one, or two, of you had reason to want Ned or Ted out of the picture.'

Bill leaned forward, knocking his glass over. 'Are you suggesting,' he said in a low voice as water pooled across the table, 'that one of us murdered Ned and Ted?'

'I'm not saying anything except that you had reasons not to like those brothers.' Rosemary held her finger up as the men started protesting. 'The fact is: both are dead.'

Thunder crashed over the house again as the men rose from the table. Mrs Lionel crouched down in her seat but Rosemary put a hand on her arm to reassure her. Once the noise had rolled away, she stood as well. 'Unless,' she said calmly, 'you have some other thoughts on the situation you'd like to share.'

Another flash of lightning, a quick follow through of angry thunder, and the lights flicked off. Rosemary felt Mrs Lionel's hand on hers. More lightning lit the house interior momentarily, and she saw that the men stayed standing, frozen in the flashes. Then the lights flickered and came on again, turning the black biker silhouettes into ordinary fellows once more.

'Well?'

Tommy scowled at Rosemary and sat down. 'I don't know if all of what you've said is true but even if it isn't, it must be one of us who did away with the twins.'

'Unless complete strangers broke into the club house,' said Bill.

'Nothing was taken. No damage was done.' Tommy shook his head. 'No one else accessed the club after we finished. Who was last to leave?'

Moose plonked down in the seat next to his brother. 'We weren't.'

'But you'd finished wrapping the older kids' presents,' said Gordy, also sitting. 'All those flat boxes. I saw you stack them ready for the sacks.'

Moose stroked his face. 'Yep, we had them ready for sure.'

'But she...' Harry stabbed a finger toward Rosemary '... she said you'd substituted books for computers!' He leaned forward, his hands on the table. 'You two are thieves! Ned and Ted found out and you silenced them.' He drew a finger across his throat.

'Rubbish,' said Tommy. 'We didn't put a finger on

them.' He glared at Bill and Rock. 'But I heard you two yelling out the back.'

Rock stiffened. 'What do you mean?'

'You were shouting at them. I couldn't hear what you were saying but you weren't singing a lullaby.'

'So, we shouted at them.' Bill fiddled with his water glass, slopping its contents on the table. 'So what? They were idiots. They wouldn't...'

'Wouldn't what?' said Harry. 'What did you ask them to do?'

'Hang on,' said Gordy, smiling viciously. 'Ted was your new accountant. He wouldn't diddle the books for you, would he?'

Bill started mopping water with a serviette and didn't look up.

Harry grinned at Bill. 'I knew there was something dodgy about you.'

Bill glared at the other man. 'And there's nothing dodgy about you?'

'What do you mean by that?'

'I know about your fake IDs.'

'*Novelty* IDs. We don't hide the fact that they aren't real.'

'Oh, but for certain people, you can add watermarks to increase their validity.'

Harry's grin dropped from his face. 'What do you know about those watermarks?'

'Ned told me.' Bill frowned. 'How did he know?'

Harry wriggled uncomfortably. 'Because he asked about them.'

'What do you mean?'

'He asked. He wanted to know if we could make fake

IDs and not get into trouble. And what it would take to make one that was undetectable from the real thing.'

'And you told him?'

'Well, yeah.'

'Because you'd done it before?'

Gordy dropped his gaze. 'Once or twice.'

'For Ned? Did you make the licence for Timothy Armstrong?'

Gordy looked up. 'Yeah, alright, we did. I don't think he used it.' He reached into his pocket and pulled out the missing licence. 'He didn't get the chance because we only gave it to him last night.'

'What did he want it for?'

Gordy shrugged. 'That's something we never ask.'

'Shifty little characters,' muttered Bill.

'Shifty, all right,' said Rock. 'It's sad they're dead and all that, but I think we'll be better off without them in the future. They weren't much chop as bikers. Too busy doing idiotic things, like hiding in those sacks to scare us.' He scratched his chin. 'All they could talk about was whether their precious motorbikes would get scratched.'

'They did keep going on about the sidecars,' Harry said, lowering himself into his chair. 'Their *vintage* sidecars. I mean, they are valuable but, as they both were coming into a lot of money from the mother, they shouldn't have been so stupid. I wonder why they bothered loaning them to us if they were going to worry so much about them. In fact, weren't they threatening to ride off with them that night instead of taking the train to the city?'

'That's fair,' said Rock, leaning over the table to eye the empty bread bowl. 'I wouldn't loan my bike to anyone. Not even you guys.' He sat.

'It was generous of them to even think about loaning their bikes,' said Harry.

'It wasn't generous,' said Gordy, his fingers drumming the table. 'The charity paid them in advance, remember?'

'They pay us a stipend for our fuel.'

'Not as much as they offered them for use of their side-cars. Sacks full of presents are a big hit with people when we ride through towns.'

'It does look good.' Harry stroked his chin. 'We don't usually take the stipend.'

'No, but Ned and Ted did. They told me.'

'That goes back to what we told you before,' said Tommy to Rosemary. 'They weren't particularly nice fellows.'

'They were very focused on money.' Bill rolled his shoulders back. 'They were pretty keen to hear what was in their mother's will and who would get what.'

'So, who were the last of us to leave?' asked Rock. 'Who were the last to see Ned and Ted?'

The six men looked at each other, their memories apparently failing.

'Does the hall have security cameras?' asked Mrs Lionel. 'I know that's the thing to do these days.'

'Not at this hall,' said Bill. 'There was no money for cameras.'

'Right,' said Rosemary. 'So, there's nothing on record to say who left the clubhouse last.'

'Nothing,' said Tommy. He looked around at the others. 'We went to the pub for a quick one after we were done, and we left Ted and Ned there, didn't we? I mean, I didn't see them leave.' He looked at the others who shook their heads. 'I reckon we all arrived for drinks at about the same time, thinking we'd left them behind.'

'Which means,' said Gordy, 'we all left the club house at the same time.'

Rosemary pushed her chair back and stood up. 'It seems you all had reasons to want Ted and Ned kept quiet, maybe so quiet that they had to die. The big question is: when you left the club house, were they dead or or were they alive?'

# TEN

Evening fell without further conversation about the demise of Ted and Ned, although the group of bikers looked troubled. Jasper turned up as Rosemary made up beds. She tried to ignore his whispered protests that having potential murderers stay the night wasn't the best idea until finally she turned to him and said, 'Would you like to stay as well?'

He glanced towards her bedroom where Sunny sat in the doorway like a furry ginger sentry, and blushed. 'Well, you know, I could...'

'You'd be on the floor,' said Rosemary, nodding towards the cat. 'Sunny has taken refuge on my bed since visitors arrived. She's quite territorial.'

'Well,' said Jasper, face blazing. 'I could manage the floor.'

'You're welcome to it. I'll make you up a bed as well.'

More thunder crashed overhead as she finished organising sleeping arrangements but the power stayed on. The men settled around the lounge, most with their boots off, signalling their intention to do nothing until morning. Mrs Lionel stood behind the kitchen counter wiping it down.

She smiled as Rosemary joined her. 'Everything alright, dear?'

'As much as they can be.'

'Any news about the road closures?'

'Last I looked, everything was about the same.' Rosemary checked outside. 'Apparently, the rain will dissipate around midnight so we might see the water levels start to recede.'

'That's the good thing about parched soil,' said Mrs Lionel. 'It does suck up any moisture quite quickly once the curtain of rain stops.' She rinsed her cloth and hung it on the draining rack. 'Anything else I can do for you?'

'You do too much for me already. How about you head home now? The others left hours ago.'

'I will. I'm quite tired. The heat knocks me around.' Mrs Lionel pushed her grey curls from her neck. 'And, whatever happens, we're hosting Christmas Day tomorrow.'

'Maybe someone will remember my favourite dessert this year.'

Mrs Lionel frowned. 'What is your favourite dessert?'

'Trifle.'

'It's a bit too late telling me that.' Mrs Lionel patted Rosemary's arm. 'See you tomorrow, dear.'

Rosemary walked Mrs Lionel to the door. The croaking of the electronic frog told Rosemary her friend had made the few steps to home.

'It's just us, then.'

Rosemary turned at Jasper's soft voice. He stood behind her, dark hair looped behind one ear, gazing out into the rain. 'Us, and six others.'

Jasper's face warmed. 'Yes, yes. I almost forgot.'

'Jasper,' said Rosemary firmly.

'I know. How could I forget?' Jasper smiled wryly. 'And

how do we keep six bikers entertained until the police get here?'

The six bikers didn't need entertaining. By the time Jasper and Rosemary went back into her living area, Bill and Rock were asleep on their backs on the floor, snoring roughly. Harry and Gordy sat on the couch, bent over a pack of cards. Tommy and Moose sat in the remaining armchairs, Tommy with one of Rosemary's cookbooks and Moose studying his phone.

Rosemary made Jasper a cup of tea and sat next to him at the table where he had the book from Mullings open. 'Reading it again?'

Jasper nodded slowly. 'I'd forgotten how complicated the plot it. So many mistaken identities. People getting confused all over the place.' He chuckled. 'I guess it would be confusing at times if you have an identical twin.' He looked at Rosemary and the smile froze on his face. 'Rosemary, what are you thinking?'

'I'm thinking of the licence we found on Ned. Timothy Armstrong.'

'What about it?'

'Harry and Gordy supplied Ned with the fake. What if Ned was preparing to change his identity?'

'Why would he do that?'

'There was a substantial estate to inherit. One that would be bigger if the other was dead. Maybe even enough to take off with and start a new life.'

'They were brothers!'

'You've just finished telling me about sibling rivalry. These brothers weren't close. They had grown up apart. They were more like *competitors*.'

'What are you suggesting, Rosemary?'

Rosemary came closer to Jasper, so close that wisps of

his hair caught on her lips as she spoke. 'What if one wanted the other dead, but it went terribly wrong and both of them ended up dead?'

Jasper stole a look around the room, but the Bearded Biker Brothers were intent on their own activities. 'They think that one of them did it.'

'Only because that seems obvious. And clearly, they don't trust each other. They all have things they'd rather have kept hidden.'

'Even if what we're thinking is true, they may still be relieved that Ted and Ned are dead.'

'Which means we still need to keep an eye on them.'

Jasper stiffened. 'Why?'

'They might try to do something they shouldn't.'

'Like what?'

Rosemary leaned back. 'That, I don't know.'

# ELEVEN

The household settled to sleep soon after. The rain
continued in bursts, obliterating the view through the glass
doors at the back of the house well before the evening light
faded completely. Rosemary retreated to her bed, followed
by the flame-faced Jasper who silently shed his clothes
down to his underpants before slipping quickly under the
sheet on top of his floor bed. Rosemary tried not to think
about her glimpse of his slim torso and the beguiling 'read in
bed' slogan on his black undies. That she'd stared long
enough to make out the words made her own face flush.

Sunny stretched herself out beside her mistress once
Rosemary had made the quick leap into pyjamas then bed.
Water ran from the gutters outside the bedroom sounding
like a quiet waterfall, and she turned her attention to its
rhythm. Snores from the Bearded Bikers pierced the
comforting sound but that didn't stop her drifting off.

The rain had stopped when she woke again. Clouds still
covered the stars for it was dark outside apart from the faint
glow of streetlights on the corner of Goldmarket Road.
Rosemary moved Sunny back a little so she could sit up.

Something had woken her but what? She strained for any noise and was rewarded with one quick jangle from the shop door that was immediately stifled by…who?

She slid from the bed, grabbing a white cotton cardigan from the bedpost to fling over her shortie pyjamas. Jasper slept on as she tiptoed past, the arm flung over his face a dark shadow in the room. Rosemary felt her way out the door, sidestepping men on the floor, and went through the shop. She peered through the blind and saw two men hurrying across Goldmarket Square towards Kelly's café.

Taking care not to let the bell ring, Rosemary squeezed through the front door and crossed the road, cursing herself for wearing the bright summer cardigan which flashed under the lights as she ran. The rain started again, a sudden, hard shower that plastered her unbraided hair against her face even as she tried to swipe it away. She ducked under the Exceptional Tree and watched as the two men entered the shop and stood over Ted and Ned's bodies.

The rain stopped. Water dripped heavily from the Tree's leaves. The skin on the back of Rosemary's neck prickled. Someone's feet shuffled on the gravel behind a span of the barricade keeping people away from the Tree's trunk. She peered around as far as she could without moving and saw a leg clad in houndstooth trousers ending in a black working boot sticking out from the woven structure. 'Roman?' she called softly.

The leg retreated, and slowly a man appeared into the light from the street, blinking away the rain running down his face. 'Ah, Rosemary.' He stopped a few metres from her. 'Rain is good, no?'

'No,' said Rosemary. 'Not this much. There's flooding already.'

'Yes.' Roman inched closer. 'Justin's dam is full to boosting.'

'Bursting,' said Rosemary automatically. 'I can imagine.' She put her head to one side. 'Does it matter if what you're carrying gets wet?'

Roman stared down at the bag cradled in his arms as if he had just noticed it. He twisted to study another tied to his back. 'Ah, my vegetables.'

'You've been gone a long time. They must have been very hard to find vegetables.'

He blinked at her again as the rain started in earnest once more. The thick black moustaches on his upper lip were so sodden, the long hairs hung vertically over his mouth. His hair, lustrous black waves in the dry, had flattened over his crown. Although a raincoat hid most of the white chef's coat he wore, the tail hanging out was dripping. He shuffled the bag in his arms. 'I have the cardoons, Rosemary.' He smiled briefly. 'I found them at last.'

Rosemary checked the men in the café. Their shadows crouched, and she saw the shapes of Christmas presents being placed into the sacks once more. She sidled up to Roman. 'Did you know that Jules is looking for you? And Patti and Gerry have been driving around to see if you're stranded. People are very worried about you.'

Roman's eyebrows rose slowly, as if the thought of the worry needed deep consideration. 'I have been-'

'-collecting vegetables. Yes. That's what the others thought but you weren't at Justin's and you're not answering your phone.'

Roman's hand went slowly to his pocket and patted it once. 'It is flat.'

'That's not the only thing that's flat,' said Rosemary, staring at Roman's head. 'What happened to you?'

'I fell in the creek.' He held up the vegie bag and Rosemary saw how soaked it was. 'I fell, then rose. I struggled to get out. I was so tired.' His bottom lip trembled. 'I thought I was to drown. I must have slept.' He looked back in the general direction of his house. 'I must get back to my Jules.'

Now Rosemary saw that it wasn't only Roman's lip trembling. He shivered all over, a little like The Exceptional Tree's leaves in a light breeze. 'Come on. Let's go to my place and get you dry. I can ring Jules and the others to let them know you're okay.'

She tugged at the bag of vegetables in his arms. He relinquished his hold, dropping his arms to his side, then startled at the sound of the door opening at Mullings. Rosemary pushed him under the cover of the Tree, putting her bag down. 'Something has happened, Rosemary?' he asked, lowering his voice as she put a finger on her lip. 'Something has happened to the spiky Kelly?'

Rosemary hid her quick smile at his description of her least favourite person in Mulbury. 'Kelly is her usual self but there are two dead men in her café. And two live men coming out, having snuck in trying not to be noticed.' She gave Roman a quick version of the day.

Roman stared at the men. 'Are they dangerous, Rosemary Exeter?'

She shrugged. 'Isn't anybody when they're threatened?'

'We should stay here and let them go.' Roman turned to move closer to the barricade, tripped over the bag of vegetables, and crashed noisily to the ground.

The men halted. 'Who is it?'

Rosemary hesitated, then stepped out into The Square at the same time as the men came towards her. She waved a hand at Roman behind her back. 'Keep down,' she hissed, hoping he could hear.

Now that the men were in the open, the light hit their grey hair and turned it orange. 'Rosemary,' said Tommy. 'What are you doing?'

'She pointed to the sacks slung over their shoulders. 'I could ask you the same question.'

Moose glanced at his brother. 'We couldn't sleep so we...'

'Went for a walk?'

'That's it.'

'Inside a café?'

'We were hungry so we thought we go where the cakes came from.'

'And there was nothing in my fridge?'

Moose shuffled his feet. 'We were really craving that delicious raspberry-'

'Shut it, Moose.' Tommy stepped toward Rosemary. 'It's none of your business why we went into that café.'

Rosemary stood her ground. 'Perhaps not.' She nodded towards the sacks. 'But you could be a little less obvious about it. I see you're trying to get rid of the evidence. I bet you thought you could get on your bikes and ride away.'

Moose gave a strangled grunt and went to run for it, stepping as he did in a puddle and sliding on its clay surface. His legs went into the air, he fell flat and lay motionless.

'Moose?' said Tommy, leaning over his brother. He turned angrily to Rosemary. 'See what you've done?'

'I didn't do anything that he hadn't already done to himself. *Yourselves.*'

Tommy dropped his sack and stepped towards her. 'Is that right? Well, you're the only one to see us doing anything.'

Perhaps the sky realised Rosemary's dilemma for as she

stood in the centre of the Square with the Exceptional Tree's branches waving wildly behind her and water streamed down her neck into her Christmas pyjamas, the rain stopped abruptly. She stood facing Tommy, arms out ready to take him on. The clouds shifted for the first time since the storms had begun, letting in a sliver of full moon light which lit the beefy man in front of her and magnified his hulking menace. Rosemary braced herself.

A shout.

Rosemary kept her eyes on Tommy. Hairs rose on the back of her neck as the shout turned into a battle cry. Someone zoomed in front of hair, striped with the light of the moon, and began flaying the man with...sticks of celery?

Rosemary dropped her arms and stepped closer. Tommy was fighting back, arms up to defend himself while trying to kick his opponent who kept up a steady action of double-handed pounding. 'Roman?'

Roman didn't turn to Rosemary, instead reaching behind him into the tote bag strapped to his back and pulling out what she guessed were two large radishes still attached to their leaves. Roman swung them simultaneously, hitting Tommy on either side of his head, making him clutch his ears and shriek. The radishes tore from their leaves and bounced across the Square's gravel, but Roman was already armed with two hefty parsnips and was using them in a way that guaranteed they'd be no good to roast on Christmas Day.

The shrieking and shouting had clearly woken the rest of Mulbury. One by one, the shops under the veranda lit up and people poured from their doors in a cacophony of frogs and jangles. Rosemary saw Mrs Lionel hurrying across the road, tying her dressing gown at the same time, and ran over to her. 'It's okay,' Rosemary said. 'Roman has it.'

'Goodness me,' said Mrs Lionel, watching the vegetable wielding chef and the cowering biker. She pointed at the prostrate form of Moose on the ground. 'Is that his brother?'

'Yes.'

'Does he need medical attention?'

'Most likely.' Rosemary shrugged. 'He slipped.'

'I see.' The older woman finished tying her cord. 'I'll check on him, will I?'

'Yes, I suppose you should.'

'And in the meantime...?'

Rosemary pulled the phone from her pocket. 'I'll text Jules to tell her Roman's turned up.'

'And then?'

Rosemary tipped her head back to look at the sky. 'The rain is clearing which means the water levels across the road should stabilise. You never know, the police could be here soon.'

'In a way, it doesn't matter.' Mrs Lionel walked toward Moose. 'I don't think these brothers will be going anywhere.'

Roman had finally run out of vegetables. Tommy knelt on the ground, his arms over his head. The other biker brothers surrounded him, looking disgusted. Roman undid the empty bag from his back and plunged it over Tommy's head at the same time as Harry grabbed his arms and held them behind him. Tommy didn't protest. His ears were probably still ringing from the radish assault.

As further clouds retreated, the other residents of Mulbury ventured into the Square to better view the situation. Jasper sidled up to Rosemary. 'Are you okay?' He stroked her hair back from her face. 'You look at bit wild.'

'Thanks, Jasper.'

Even in the white moonlight, Jasper's red face glowed. 'It suits you. Really. Your hair...'

'Is a mess.' Rosemary slipped a hair tie from her wrist, combed her hair out, and started braiding, all while keeping an eye on Mrs Lionel and the now groaning Moose, who was recovering from his fall. Two bikers crouched beside him and heaved him to his feet, marching him unsympathetically to The Preserved Mulbury. 'I suppose I'd better go.'

'Can I do anything useful?' Jasper asked.

She smiled at him. 'Would you mind taking the sacks back into Mullings? And check on Ned and Ted.'

'Check on Ned and Ted? Are you sure? I mean, they won't be going anywhere.'

'Clearly. Just make sure they're covered up.'

Jasper nodded. 'Give them a bit of dignity.'

Rosemary gave Jasper's arm a squeeze. 'That's right. It's bad enough being dumped unceremoniously on a café floor. Don't touch anything if you can help it. Use Kelly's tablecloths.'

'I beg your pardon?' Kelly appeared out of the shadows of the Exceptional Tree. 'Use my tablecloths for what?'

Rosemary didn't answer but pointed instead to the open door of Mullings of Mulbury.

Kelly glanced back at her café. 'Oh, right.' She caught Jasper's arm as he went to go. 'Use the ones I'd already got out. They're old and not worth anything.' She glared at Rosemary. 'Well, I'll lose it, won't I, when the police get here.'

Rosemary shook her head and was saved by saying anything else by Mrs Lionel's approach.

'Geoffrey just texted, dear,' the older woman said.

'They hope to be here by morning. He said to keep the men contained until then.'

'We won't have any problems with that.' Rosemary pointed to Moose, who was being steered by the brothers to follow Tommy back to her shop. 'I doubt that the rest of the Bearded Brothers would let them out of their sight.'

A screech of tyres made them all turn to Goldmarket Road. Jules flung herself out of the car and ran towards Roman, white silk nightie flapping at her ankles and blonde hair tumbling down her back. The chef's walrus moustache wobbled when he saw his wife and he ran to meet her half-way. They clung to each other. Rosemary turned away at the intimate scene and noticed that others had done the same. She caught Mrs Lionel's eye. 'I guess we'll all be here for Christmas lunch.'

Mrs Lionel poked her foot at a parsnip lying battered on the gravel. 'And how wonderful that will be.'

# TWELVE

A police car roared into the Square early Christmas morning, followed by a more sedate ambulance that manoeuvred carefully up the gutter. Kelly waved to the vehicles and indicated her café. The Bearded Biker Brothers gathered under the veranda, Tommy and Moose stuck firmly in their midst. Rosemary was relieved to see Geoffrey step out of the police car, followed by two uniformed constables. She went to the door and opened it.

'Hello, Rosemary.' The older detective shook his head at her. 'More bodies? They really do pile up in Mulbury.'

'Hello, Geoffrey. Maybe we know you like it here?'

'Hmph. I'd like it better if it wasn't always the scene of a crime. Now, let's see what you've got.'

Geoffrey directed his colleagues to the café as Rosemary explained yesterday's events. 'I see,' he said. 'And do you have some idea of why two bikers ended up dead in sacks full of Christmas presents?'

'I have some thoughts on the matter. Your team may arrive at different conclusions.'

The older police officer grunted. 'I doubt it. They

haven't before. Alright, I'll come and see you later to talk further.' He strode to the café.

It was late morning, and the turkey roll in the oven filled the house with tantalising Christmas lunch fragrance, before the roar of motorbikes filled the shop. Rosemary watched through the window as two police vehicles escorted six motorbikes back to Big Town, leaving two bikes and their sidecars behind. Quiet settled on The Preserved Mulbury, the soft hum of Christmas carols playing in her lounge room filtering out to fill the space.

Jasper walked softly up behind her, the creak of floorboards heralding his progress. He stood next to her and gazed out at the busy Square. 'Are you alright, Rosemary?' he asked.

'Yes. I'm good.' She shrugged. 'As good as you can be knowing there are two dead brothers within cooee.'

'Yeah, horrible. Not nice on Christmas Day.' He took her hand and squeezed it before letting it go. 'Thanks for letting me stay in your, ah, bedroom.'

She glanced at him, noting the crimson glow. 'These were exceptional circumstances.'

'Well,' he said. 'If exceptional circumstances arise again, I'd be happy...you know...'

Rosemary was saved from answering by Geoffrey jangling in the door tailed by a young constable. 'Rosemary,' he said. 'Jasper.'

'Come in,' Rosemary asked. 'You'll need a drink.'

Geoffrey took a handkerchief from his pocket and wiped his forehead. 'Thank you. The rain's stopped and now the sun is beating down. That's more like the Christmas Day we expect.'

'We'll be back in drought before you know it,' said Jasper cheerily.

The detective shook his head. 'Let's hope not.'

'Oh,' said Jasper. 'I didn't mean...'

But Geoffrey was following Rosemary into the cool of the house and had spotted an old friend. 'Ah, Mrs Lionel,' he said, smiling. 'There you are.'

'Hello, Geoffrey,' she said. 'It seems we have a Christmas pickle for you.'

'Two Christmas pickles,' said the detective. 'It's getting busier around here.' He spotted the fare on Rosemary's dining room table. 'Christmas nibbles,' he said, and then seemed to remember his charge.

'You will stop for a break,' said Mrs Lionel. 'Surely you have time for that.'

Geoffrey glanced at his colleague. 'Yes, I do. We're waiting for them to be finished with the deceased. The Bearded Biker Brothers were sent to Big Town's police station where we'll take initial witness statements. That's all we can do for now.' He glanced at Rosemary. 'Except to listen to what you have to say.'

'Eat up.' Mrs Lionel waved a butter knife at Rosemary. 'I'll get Jasper to take some over to the team at Kelly's.'

'Thank you,' said Geoffrey, dismissing the constable with a nod and settling on a dining chair. 'That's kind of you. Okay, Rosemary. Talk.'

Rosemary settled in a chair and indicated Geoffrey should do the same. 'Ted and Ned O'Reilly were found dead in the sacks when Tommy and Moose dumped them in Kelly's café.'

Geoffrey sat, nodding.

'The brothers were recently united, having been separated at birth. They were both recipients of their mother's substantial estate, and that was how they discovered each other.'

'Okay.'

'Separately, each would have inherited the lot if the other was also dead.'

'Are you saying...?'

Rosemary sat down at the table. 'They had identical pill containers in their pockets. My guess would be that they contained the same brand of sleeping tablets. I think they'd both given each other a large dose which was why they were both sleepy.'

'Large enough to kill them?'

Rosemary shook her head. 'The scum on Ted's lips indicates a drug overdose of some kind but it wasn't from too many sleeping tablets. I think you'll find that the orange juice his brother was offering was more than fruit juice.'

'Poison?'

'Ned knew how to buy chemicals, even those not usually used to clean houses.'

'And the other one?'

'Ted had a hanky that smelled like dry cleaning fluid but I've never known anyone who dry cleaned their handkerchiefs. I suspect there was chloroform on the hanky. One of Ted's clients was a laboratory he regularly visited, so he may have taken some from there.'

'He knocked out his own brother?'

'It wouldn't have been hard because the sleeping tablets had already done some of the work. The wad of paper in Ned's mouth kept his mouth full so all Ted had to do was cover his nose.'

'And they did all this while in the sacks?'

Rosemary shrugged. 'What better place? I can imagine one brother enticing the other to do that stunt of scaring the remaining Biker Brothers, with the intent of having a dead body neatly hidden away once the deed was done.'

'But neither of them made it.' Geoffrey nodded thought-fully. 'But we can't rule out it could be that the other men that murdered them.'

'THE OTHER MEN didn't like the twins, for various reasons that you'll find out. But they didn't have the means or the opportunity to murder them.'

'So...?'

'Ted and Ned murdered each other.'

Geoffrey nodded slowly. 'This will need a lot of inves-tigation.'

Rosemary folded her hands together on the table. 'I told you your team wouldn't like it.'

'When will you know the full extent of what happened?' Mrs Lionel asked, placing a large glass of punch in front of Geoffrey before sitting next to Rosemary.

'A good while.' Geoffrey selected a mince pie from the plate and took a large bite. 'If ever.' He chewed thought-fully. 'These are good pies.'

'Aunt Lilibeth's mince recipe,' said Rosemary, indi-cating the old recipe book on her shelf.

Geoffrey finished his pie and drained his glass. 'Once again, I need to thank everyone for their help.' He stood up. 'I best go back. Have a Merry Christmas.'

'And you.' Mrs Lionel handed the police officer a wrapped package with more pies. 'Take these for later.'

Geoffrey took it with a nod. 'Thank you.' He tipped his head at Rosemary. 'Keep dry.'

Rosemary stood to watch him go out the door and head back to the busy scene across the road. 'I'm not sure he believes me.'

'Geoffrey will believe what gets proven. If that's your

theory, then once again he has you to thank for providing leads.'

Rosemary said nothing, saved by the scurrying figure of Rakisha heading across the Square to The Preserved Mulbury. She flung in the door carrying a container. 'Oh, darling Rosemary,' she said as she flounced through to the lounge area. 'I've bought your favourite Christmas dessert.'

'I don't think you make my favourite Christmas dessert,' said Rosemary, eyeing the container that was now on its side as Rakisha shed her cardigan.

'I do, darling. You've always said you liked my granola.'

'What I said was that your granola is the most edible substance in your café.'

Rakisha blinked a few times, then shook her head. 'See, it is your favourite! So, I made granola trifle.' She thrust the container at Rosemary, its contents sliding sloppily around in it.

'I don't-'

'Thank you, dear,' said Mrs Lionel, taking the container from Rakisha's outstretched hand and elbowing Rosemary at the same time. 'We appreciate the effort you've put into Christmas lunch.'

Rakisha nodded, her feathered earrings tangling in her hair. 'Thank you, Mrs Lionel, darling. You so understand the goodness in my organic gifts from Mother Earth.'

Mrs Lionel took Rakisha's arm and steered her to the couch. 'Have a ginger cordial and sit down in the cool.'

While Mrs Lionel sat with Rakisha, Rosemary pried the lid from the container and winced at its grey contents. She put the lid back on and slid it to the furthest corner of the fridge. As she straightened, Jules and Roman came into the room. 'At least you will have brought something delicious,' she said as Roman set a casserole dish carefully onto the bench.

'It is more than delicious,' he said. 'It is tradition.'

Rosemary studied him closely. The trials of the last twenty-four hours were still on his pale face, but the smile was back behind the heavy moustaches and he looked more like the Roman of old than he had for weeks. 'What happened, Roman? Why were you so sad?'

Jules stepped forward and took her husband's arm. 'It was his mother's death, Rosemary.'

'Understandable,' said Rosemary. 'But there was something else, wasn't there?'

Roman's moustaches quivered. 'It was my duty,' he said softly, 'to continue the tradition and I found myself bereft of this particular vegetable. I was very sad but the good farmer Justin came to the rescue. He procured the vegetable for me and I was very grating.'

'Grateful,' said Jules automatically.

Roman lifted the casserole lid and Rosemary leaned over to peer in at the succulent green dish. 'Cardoons, dear Rosemary. I have been in search for months.'

'Do I recognise that vegetable from your heroics this morning?'

Roman nodded solemnly. 'I was able to utilise them appropriately.' He mimed two long stalks whacking an imaginary man.

'They hold up well, then. And now you've found them, you can make your mother's traditional dish?'

'Which I have done. And which will now be known as Capriccio's Cardoons.'

Jules squeezed his arm again. 'Which we'll have every Christmas as long as Justin can get them for us.'

'It is full circle.' Roman sighed, putting the lid on the dish and patting it.

The door jangled again. 'Oh, look, Gerry! Roman's here and doesn't he look gorgeous?'

Gorgeous was not the description Rosemary had ever applied to Roman, but Patti ran forward and folded her arms around the chef, clearly finding his gorgeousness compelling.

'Ah, Roman.' Gerry hurried forward and shook Roman's outstretched hand vigorously. 'You gave us a real fright. Patti and I searched the roads as far as we could go, but the water was too high. We feared for you.'

Roman extracted himself from Gerry's wife and nodded solemnly. 'I feared for myself.'

'But it's all good.' Patti looked at Jules who smiled. 'It's all good now.' She clapped her hands together and rocked from side to side, making her swing dress sway. 'And I can smell such a delicious lunch, Rosemary! We've brought trifle.'

Rosemary grimaced. 'It's not made of granola, is it?'

Patti's puzzled look was cut short by further jangling at the door. This time it was Jasper returning from his mission to feed the investigators. He sought out Rosemary. 'They're going.'

The mob of Mulburians moved to The Preserved Mulbury's windows to watch. Ambulance officers loaded Ned and Ted into their vehicles, and the body bags shone in the bright sunshine. Someone carried the sacks out in large evidence bags, followed by others carrying the rest of the evidence. That loaded, the team drove off. Geoffrey and his constables stepped from the café last of all, watched by Kelly as he shut the door and blocked it with crime tape. She raised her arms in protest but Geoffrey didn't stop. He marched across the Square with his young colleagues trailing behind him, climbed into his car, and was driven away.

'I'll get her,' said Jasper.

'Who?' asked Rosemary.

'Kelly.'

'Right.'

'She needs to come in and have lunch with us, dear.' Mrs Lionel brushed her hands on her apron. 'And we need to get busy serving it.'

Rosemary's phone rang, a light cheerful rendition of Jingle Bells. She looked at Mrs Lionel.

'That's your daughter, dear, so answer it.' Mrs Lionel moved to the kitchen. 'I'll get started.'

Rosemary stayed in her shop as the others followed the older woman and answered the call. 'Honey Blossom.'

Honey's voice sounded far away, the crash of waves from her holiday destination distinct in the background. 'Mum, Merry Christmas! How is it in Mulbury? Quiet, I imagine.'

Rosemary turned to look out the window. Blue and white crime tape flapped lazily from Kelly's café, and the proprietor herself was having some sort of hissy fit in the Square while Jasper stood trying to soothe her with a hand rubbing her arm. A flock of cockatoos chose that moment to swoop from The Exceptional Tree, filling the air with raucous squawks, frightening pink and white galahs who took off from where they were pecking at the sodden gravel in the Square, shrieking madly.

She smiled and brought her attention back to the phone. 'Quiet? Yes. As quiet as Mulbury ever is.'

## Mulbury Mysteries

Small-town cosies featuring quirky residents and an unimpressed cat!

### A Sticky Situation: #1 Mulbury Mystery

When Mrs Lionel discovers the body of an old man under The Exceptional Tree, everyone in the town of Mulbury assumes that he died peacefully. Everyone, that is, except Rosemary who doesn't think the old man's death was particularly peaceful, not when no one has ever seen the man before in a town where everyone knows everyone else.

### A Pretty Pickle: #2 Mulbury Mystery

When Jasper Lu uncovers a skeleton in his back yard, the town suddenly becomes much busier. The police arrive, followed closely by Adelia Lochard the filmmaker and Rosemary's son-in-law, Ronnie the private investigator. Then come people Rosemary has never seen before: a handsome man in a worn leather jacket, a loud and happy family of mudlarkers, and two women claiming to be the daughters of an old resident. In all this, the skeleton remains a mystery until more than bones are dug up from Mulbury's past.

### A Tricky Treat: #3 Mulbury Mystery

Spring in Mulbury, and the Gala is in full swing. Rosemary

Exeter's pickles and marmalades are selling briskly at her stall, alongside Mrs Lionel's green cleaning products and Jasper Lu's secondhand books – until there are screams from across the road. By the time Rosemary gets there, it's to discover Mrs Caroline King, matriarch of a cattle empire, tipped over in her wheelchair gasping for breath on the gravel of Goldmarket Square.

## One Christmas Pickle: a Mulbury Mystery Novella

What if Santa came to town and promptly dropped dead? Rosemary Exeter has a couple of mysteries on her mind. Who is the Kris Kringle leaving presents hanging from everyone's door handles and, more gravely, who overcooked the fire brigade's fund-raising Santa? With the team of fire-fighting volunteers stuck in Mulbury until their truck is fixed, and almost certainly one of them a murderer, Rosemary hides the one clue she has while searching for others.

## ABOUT THE AUTHOR

Juno Harvey lives in Victoria, Australia, with her family. She makes jam on the weekends and works in a university during the week.

Want to join Juno's Reader's Team?
Click here (or go to www.junoharvey.com) and receive a free book!

https://www.junoharvey.com/

Books of light...and shade.